RILEY'S EXCELLENT AND NOT-AT-ALL FAKE EXORCISM SERVICE

Sophie Queen

ISBN-9798687288361

Front Cover Image By: Anh Nguyen
Cover design by: Anh Nguyen
Library of Congress Control Number: 2018675309
Printed in the United States of America

For my Mom,
I'm sorry for all the cursing.

PREFACE

Well . . . Fuck

"This can't be real." He told himself, "You've just had too much to drink. It was a long day. Come on, man. Come on."

Music and idle chatter surrounded him as he hurriedly made his way to the mansion's front doors. A butler in a neat tux tried to ask him if he needed his jacket, but he was in too much of a hurry to hear him, let alone respond. Once outside, his quick pace turned into a sprint, across the large perfectly manicured lawn to the street, which was lined with high-end cars. Down, until he reached his house. The *Sold* sign was still placed out front. He ran inside, passing boxes they had yet to unpack, and dashed straight upstairs to the bedroom.

His back was pressed against the mahogany door. He wiped his brow while taking in a heavy breath and walked over to the mini-bar by the balcony window, where he poured himself a generous amount of amber liquor from the crystal decanter.

"Just one more drink, then you'll go to sleep." He gripped the glass in his trembling hand, between gulps of as much liquor as his throat would allow. "You didn't see what you think you saw." He chanted this over and over, until his heartbeat turned from a relentless beating to a steadier rhythm. He removed his phone from his suit jacket, opening it to Erica's number, but hesitated to call. He glanced over at the king-sized bed, covered in its crisp satin sheets. Just this morning, they were there together, tumbling around in sweet marital bliss.

"Stop it," he scolded himself, "Everything's fine. This is your new house, your new life. You're safe here. Erica will be back and she'll laugh at you for running out of the party like that. Yeah, she'll come back here . . . she'll be . . . normal." He polished off his drink, removed his jacket and tossed it on the lounge chair next to the bar. He walked into the bathroom connected to his and Erica's bedroom. Looking in the mirror, it took a second for him to recognize himself. His face was flushed, his pupils dilated to the point that they looked almost black.

He turned on the faucet, splashed water over his face, his neck. With his eyes closed, he repeated over and over. *"This can't be real . . ."*

That was when he heard the bedroom door open . . . *slowly*.

"Tommy?" It was Erica. But her voice, it sounded off,

distant and cold. Not what he was used to. "You're here, aren't you, Tommy?"

The large door slammed shut. The room around him seemed to grow colder with every click of Erica's heels. He listened as she crossed the bedroom toward him. Glancing in the mirror, he peered at his reflection again. He was trembling. His eyes were still as black as the night sky. He tried to speak, but all that came out was a weak whimper.

"Tommy," From the corner of his eye, he saw her silhouette leaning against the door frame. "Why did you run away, Tommy?"

He didn't look at her. He couldn't.

"Look at me, Tommy," she commanded, her voice wasn't the kind, energetic one he knew. That he loved. This voice was cruel, full of distance. This was the voice of a stranger. "We're going to get everything, Tommy. Everything we've ever wanted."

"E-Erica," he sputtered, through chattering teeth. It was so cold. "This isn't real. I-it can't be."

"Oh, sweet Tommy," she said, chuckling. "This is so very real. More real than anything before. You'll see, you'll understand . . . soon."

"E-Erica," He mustered all the courage that remained within him and looked at her. But it wasn't her. No, not entirely. He stumbled back. His skin turned the color of fresh snow. He couldn't move his arms, hands or fingers. It was as if they had turned to ice. His eyes widened, turning even darker. *Black.*

His mind was unable to process what was before him.

All he could say was, "Well . . . Fuck."

CHAPTER ONE

Writer's Juice

Fifteen floors below me, cars and people hustled down the long city streets. The air was damp, thick and rich with the scent of car fumes and soiled dreams. The cigarette between my lips did little to quell the dark imposing forces dancing in the back of my mind.

No, that was what my black coffee spiked with Irish whiskey was for. Or as I liked to call it, my writer's juice.

Though, in all honesty, writer's juice was always just whatever I was drinking at the time. Spiked coffee was just my morning writer's juice. At lunch, I'd switch to beer, or usually two. Maybe even a shot of tequila on a particularly bad day, always followed by generous amounts of mouthwash. And as the evening approached, wine while I cooked dinner, then another glass with dinner, and whiskey neat to end the day.

My husband, Daniel, only knew about the two glasses of wine and the nightcap. He'd often have them with me. One time though, he came home for lunch to surprise me, and that had been a particularly bad day, so he found me buzzed on the couch with a bottle of tequila and slices of lime. That was probably one of the worst fights we'd ever had. I told him I'd never do it again.

But really, I just learned to be more careful.

He didn't get it. I worked from home. I was a freelance editor. He's never had to deal with writers before. They're temperamental. Incapable of keeping a solid schedule. And worst of all, he didn't understand having to work for people that had everything you want, yet they didn't even know the difference between "then" and "than". I had tried for years to publish my book. Despite all the authors whose crap I polished and slaved over till they turned into mother fucking diamonds; my own dream still eluded me.

"It's just not marketable."

"Can't you write YA?"

"Maybe a romance?"

Pricks.

The pay was pretty much shit, too. I didn't make nearly enough to afford our comfortable Manhattan one-bedroom apartment. That's what my Daniel was for. But I did make enough for food, liquor, and the occasional splurge on a good book. I knew, deep down, that Daniel wished I had a better job, that I wasn't home all day.

I couldn't count on one hand the number of times he's suggested I take a yoga class, a cooking class, volunteer – anything where I would leave the apartment and just socialize. But I had my cat, and I had a best friend. Andrea was the only person from high school that ever knew I existed. And honestly, that was all I needed.

Daniel had always been surrounded by family and friends, but I was used to being alone. My upbringing was a tale told far too often. Dad left before I could even form a memory, and my mother worked multiple jobs to put food on our plates. She died before I graduated high school. Breast cancer. At her funeral, I didn't even cry. I looked at her in that cheap casket, cold and pale, her face dolled up more than it ever had been when she was alive, all I kept thinking was,

I never even knew you.

I took another drag. Followed by a gulp of my writer's juice. The coffee was lukewarm, but the whiskey still burned the back of my throat. I glanced back at my desk. Visible through the glass doors to the balcony was my cat, in all her fluffy orange glory, curled up neatly on top of my computer keyboard.

I closed my eyes.

The image of the email I had received a few minutes ago resurfaced.

Riley,

I've looked over your manuscript, and even with this rewrite, I just don't feel this is the right project for me

to take on. I hope you understand. If you ever decide to work on something else, perhaps in a different genre, you know I would be happy to look it over.

I wish you all the best,

Rebecca

I downed the rest of my beverage.

It was barely nine, but I walked over to my closet and opened the suitcase tucked near the back, under a pile of clothing, revealing my secret liquor stash. I popped open a bottle of red. Beer just wasn't going to cut it. Deciding to keep things a little classy, I grabbed a wine glass and filled it to the brim before heading out to the balcony once more. I extracted a new cigarette, the one vice I didn't have to hide from Daniel. Both of us had black lungs, for sure. I lit up.

Fuck Rebecca. *Fuck* her. She had given me so much hope. Though I knew it was just because she didn't want to lose me. I'd worked with her and a few of her clients for years; I was cheap and efficient. So, she had humored me. She went through my manuscript, told me some things I needed to work on. Said she'd talk to some people. In my heart of hearts, I already knew she wouldn't take me on. She worked with best sellers. And I . . . I wasn't one.

"Stop trying to write the next great American novel," she said to me once at lunch. She had two more glasses of wine than she normally would. "People hardly read anymore, Riley. And when they do, they want something fun! Write something for young adults, Riley. For teens. Something with a love triangle. Hell, even throw in vampires or something! No one wants to read about a woman in her late twenties who's mildly depressed. I mean, nothing really *happens* in your book. There's no cheating husband. No twists. No turns. No mystery. Nothing that wants to make you turn the page. Your book's way too slow and long. People want short, exciting, fantastical."

"I want my book to be meaningful. I want people to relate and understand what my character's going through. I know it's not for everyone . . ."

"Riley, you've worked in this industry for seven years now," she said, as she downed the rest of her drink. "Honestly, who is your book even for?"

After that, she asked me if I thought about what she said. If I made some changes. Cut it down. At the very least, have my character's husband cheating on her and she would see what she could do. So I did. Everything she said. Even though it didn't feel right, I did it.

Cut to today, to that email, to me pouring a second glass of wine.

I wasn't going to work today. I didn't really need to. I had been on top of everything all week; there were a few things I could do to get a head start for next week. Things I had planned to do but the email ruined that plan. So, I made a new plan. I was going to get drunk. Maybe order a pizza and garlic knots, lots and lots of garlic knots.

Daniel was on a business trip. He had left early that morning, before I had even woken up. He wouldn't be back till Tuesday. Off to his company's office in California, he'd be playing golf and drinking martinis all weekend, enjoying the nice, warm weather while I was here. Stuck in cold, wet Manhattan.

He had offered to bring me along, but I hated his coworkers. Besides, I seriously doubted any of his colleagues would bring their wives. His company was ninety percent male and most of them acted more like frat boys than professional businessmen. Daniel told me he hated them, too. But I know he didn't. I knew he loved golf, martinis, socializing.

When we first got married, I used to worry about him becoming like them. I knew they often went to "Gentlemen's Clubs", and that a lot of them were cheating on their wives. I used to worry Daniel would cheat on me as well, but he always came home at night. He never smelled like another woman. His phone was never locked, and he never flinched or tried to stop me from using his laptop.

So, as far as I could tell, he had never cheated.

And I decided long ago that if he did, and was this good at hiding it, then I should just let him keep on keeping on. What you don't know can't hurt you. And besides, I knew he loved me enough to look over my many flaws and icy cold exterior. What more could I ask for, really?

And with Daniel, I got a nice cozy apartment in Manhattan.

It wasn't a big apartment, but it was nicer than anything I could ever get on my own. I had always dreamed of living in the city. I think it's part of the whole writers' fantasy, one I was still trying to live fully. New Jersey-born, after my mother died, I started working at the Princeton library. I never would have been able to go there, as I didn't have the money or grades. But at the time, I just felt lucky to be there and to be surrounded by books.

I wasn't a remarkable employee, but I didn't steal books, I showed up on time, and I had a passable customer service smile. I was there for years. I read and wrote more back then than I do now. I was full of stories in my youth. None of them were that good, but I wrote them down anyway. The small apartment my uncle Vinnie owned and let me rent for a discount, more because he felt bad for me than because he actually liked me, was full of books and journals filled to the brim with my scribblings.

I was happy back then, or as happy as I could have been capable, though I was pretty lonely. My uncle didn't allow pets in his apartment building, and Andrea was at a college about two hours away, working toward her nursing degree. She was busy and stressed. I was lucky if I saw her once every month or so. I was twenty when I met Daniel. He was eighteen and a freshman at Princeton. He was going to be a hotshot lawyer. I was a poor librarian with a pipe dream.

To this day, I couldn't say why he fell for me. His parents certainly didn't approve. Both came from Poland and were hard-working people who wanted the best life possible for their son. They ran a small restaurant in Pennsylvania. I was never a fan of Polish food or Pennsylvania. But to this day, I've never told Daniel that. And over time, his parents learned to tolerate me.

The first time they met me, they asked if any of my

family came from Poland. I have blonde hair and green eyes, so they had some hope. But even if I had, I don't think that would have made them like me any better. I spent a few years trying to learn Polish. But I sucked, so I quit. His mother wasn't too happy about that.

Now they hated me because I was two years from thirty, and never gave them the fair-haired grandchildren they so desperately wanted. Every dinner now, that's all they talked about. Daniel and I never really talked about it ourselves. But around them, he always said we would soon. Once we were more financially stable. Once we moved out of Manhattan. Got a real house, with a white picket fence.

Cut to me pouring glass number three.

My phone buzzed. I looked at the screen and a smile formed on my lips.

"Andrea!" I said into the phone.

"Brunching this morning?" she asked.

"Why are you asking?"

"You sound happy, so you must be drinking," she sounded amused, which was good. If it had been Daniel, I would have gotten a lecture.

"Well. Can it still be considered brunch if it's red wine and there's no food involved?"

"Riley, Riley," I could picture her shaking her head, with a large grin on her face. "I'm picking up bagels, I have champagne and orange juice as well. Be there in like, fifteen? Maybe less."

"And when did I invite you over?"

"I just worked an unbelievably stressful twelve hours! I need drinks! And lots of them! Any complaints?"

"Nope. None."

"Good."

I listened as she hung up. I took another hefty sip of my drink...

"Ah," I held up my glass and smiled. "Writer's Juice."

CHAPTER TWO

Well . . . Ain't All This Just Fine and Dandy

You wouldn't think it was possible for someone like me, who drinks perpetually. nonstop, to get hungover. Yet there I was, legs dangling off the couch, with a head that felt like it was about to split open. With my throat so dry, I could hardly manage a swallow, and my cat perched on my belly, looking down at me with judgmental eyes.

"Don't look at me like that." I grumbled, as I placed her next to me on the couch. "Don't you have anything better to do? Like lick your butthole or whatever." I glanced over at the remnants of pizza, wine bottles, and the cause of my suffering, a bone-dry bottle of tequila.

My one and only frenemy.

The moment I managed to stand; I knew I was done for.

The room spun as I ran, barely making it to the sink before pure evil thrust its way from my throat. Hot chunks of pizza and bad decisions splattered all over the sink.

Behind me, I heard someone approach. In my state, I had a moment of panic. *Shit! Daniel's home?* He hated when I got so fucked up that I threw up. To be fair, I didn't like it either. But I wouldn't yell at someone who was puking their brains out. Daniel would. But much to my relief, when I looked behind me, it was a glowing caramel-skinned goddess, and not my husband. I could tell from the bags under her large, ebony eyes that Andrea wasn't feeling too hot herself. Even so, she looked stunning as always. Her curvy figure filling out one of my pajamas sets better than my stick-like frame ever could. Her long, thick, perfectly highlighted hair was expertly tied up in the most immaculate of messy buns.

"Daniel called you." She handed me my phone; I must have been charging it in my bedroom. "I told him you'd call him back."

After saying that, she wobbled over to the bathroom.

I was feeling much better. It's amazing what a good puke can accomplish. I started a pot of coffee before I called Daniel back. I couldn't keep Andrea un-caffeinated for very long, not if I wanted to live to see thirty. I took a deep breath before tapping his name on my phone. After two rings, he picked up.

"Morning, darling." The sugary tone in his voice confused me. If he had spoken to Andrea, he must be aware we drank last night. Honestly, I was expecting him to start with the questions right away. How much did you drink? Is the apartment a mess? Did you do anything productive yesterday?

"Morning," I hated the way my voice cracked. *Buck up, Riley!* I scolded myself.

"So, don't hate me," he said in his *I'm cute, don't be mad at me* voice.

"And why might I possibly hate you?"

"First, I want to say I had no idea this was happening. If I did, I never would have gone on my business trip. And second, I want to reiterate that you are the best wife any man could ask for. And I love you very much."

Okay, now I was scared.

Did he hook up with a stripper or something?

"My parents called me this morning with a, um . . . " I didn't know what was more terrifying, the long-outdrawn pause, or the fact this had something to do with his parents, "some interesting news."

Ooh, boy.

"Your silence is making me nervous," he said, chuckling.

"How long it's taking you to tell me what's going on is making *me* nervous," I countered in the least sassy way my hung-over self could muster.

"Fair enough, no more theatrics." I heard him clearing his throat. "So my parents moved . . . to New York."

I felt like someone slapped me in the face. I felt like I wanted to throw up, again.

I didn't hate his parents, not at all. But I liked that they lived two hours away. It was just far enough that we didn't have to see them when we didn't want to, but close enough for the times when we did.

"Not . . . in Manhattan," I said this more as a statement than a question. From what I'd seen, I couldn't imagine them having nearly enough to afford a city apartment.

"No . . . no, of course not." He sounded a little put-off but bounced back quickly. "They're just outside the city. I looked up the address and it was about forty minutes away from us. They said it's a nice little gated community."

Okay, okay that's not bad. It's a little closer than I would like. It means we'll probably have to have more family dinners. But it wasn't like they were next door or anything.

"So wait, when are they moving?" I poured myself a cup of coffee.

"No, they moved. They're there already, apparently. They wanted it to be a surprise, I guess."

"Oh." That was it, that was all I could muster.

"They wanted to have dinner with us tonight."

"Ah,"

"I'm sorry to ask this, but could you go? They didn't know I was out of town . . . and it sounded like they had this fancy dinner planned." He genuinely sounded sorry; he knew

I needed a buffer when it came to his parents. "You can bring Andrea if she's not busy. My dad's always liked her. And I don't think they'll bring up the whole kids thing if she's with you."

They probably would.

"Yeah, I'll go." I gave in. A quick dinner; I could survive that. "Send me the address?"

"You're the best, seriously," He sounded relieved; so much so, that a small part of me felt a bit offended. I mean sure this was last minute and more than a little inconvenient. But did he really think I'd be so opposed to having dinner with his parents? "Pick them up a nice housewarming gift before you go. Maybe get that bottle of scotch my dad likes, Mom would probably want something cute for the kitchen. I can send you some ideas."

"I think I can handle shopping." It came off snippier than I had meant. "What time do I have to be there?"

"Mom said seven. Text her and tell her you're excited, yeah? And once you know if Andrea's coming or not, let her know."

"I will."

"I love you," he said in that cutesy tone again.

"Yeah, I love you too." I hung up and grabbed the Irish whiskey bottle from the liquor cabinet and poured a generous amount into my coffee.

"Give me some of that!" Andrea had emerged from the bathroom with fresh makeup and perfect beach waves in her hair. How long had I been on the phone? What, less than five minutes?

I poured her coffee and added the whiskey.

"There's coffee creamer in the fridge," I said, handing her the mug.

"Please tell me it's Dulce de Leche," she said, as she dashed to the fridge.

"Not sure, you know I don't drink that shit." The only thing I liked in my coffee was whiskey, never was a fat-free, double caramel pump, extra shot of espresso, latte type of gal.

From the fridge, she extracted the plain old French Vanilla creamer. She used it anyway, even though disappointment was painted across her full, pouty lips.

"So, what did your hubby want?" she asked, resting her curvaceous thigh against the counter.

"Great news!" I said, a bit too forcefully. "My in-laws moved less than an hour away."

“Really?” She raised her brow in surprise. “And you're just finding out about this?”

“Yep,” I grumbled. “Apparently, Daniel didn't even know, they wanted it to be a *surprise*.”

"Well, your daddy-in-law's always been a sweetie," she said encouragingly. "And he's pretty cute."

I flashed her a look.

"I meant for an older man." She looked off to the side, taking another sip of her coffee. Andrea had never had good taste in men. Now, she's only ever actually had three boyfriends, all of which she was determined would be 'the one'. And to her credit, none of the three had been bad guys by any stretch of the imagination. But she had gone on many dates with a lot of losers and had even more crushes that perplexed me to no end.

Despite her near goddess-tier looks and successful nursing career, she had a 'why not give them a shot' attitude that often put her in a bad spot. She's had two stalkers, both with restraining orders now, and that's only counting the ones that bothered her in real life. She's constantly getting weird messages and dick pics from strangers online, although that never seemed to faze her. She wasn't Instafamous per se, but she did well, she even got sponsorships every now and again. Her brand basically being, "Look, I'm hot and a nurse, and I go to church every Sunday."

Why she's my friend, I would never really know.

But I wasn't complaining.

"They want me to come to their new place for dinner tonight," I said, sipping my own beverage that was bordering on room temperature.

"Do they need help moving?"

"All moved in, apparently." I poured more coffee and whiskey into my mug. "Can you come with? To dinner, I mean."

"Hmmm." She appeared to be mulling over the situation in her pretty little head.

"I mean, since my father-in-law's so cute and all," I

interrupted her thoughts with that little jab, hoping to God it was enough to convince her to go.

"Well, I guess," she chuckled. "Can't let you go off to the wolves alone, now can I?"

"Thank you!" I said with a sigh, relief washing over me.

"This isn't going to be a sleepover situation, right?" She polished off her coffee, then poured another. "I have to take my abuela to church."

I made a gun with my fingers and pointed it at my head.

"Trust me, we'll be there an hour or two, tops." There was no way I was staying over, especially without Daniel. "We'll eat, I'll help with the cleanup, and then we're out of there."

"Okay, I'm down!" she smiled brightly. "But I'm gonna need to swing by my place for an outfit change."

"Sounds good." I beamed.

"There's one condition though!" She paused, touching her a perfectly manicured finger to her face. "You have to take pictures for me. Anywhere and everywhere I want. Deal?"

"Deal!"

***

After swinging by Andrea's place and shopping for welcome gifts, we had a few hours to kill so we had a late lunch and cocktails and I took so many pictures of her that my fingers started to cramp. It was ten to six when we hopped in her car. Traffic was bad as per usual, but according to the GPS, we were on track to make it there on time.

"Lilith's Gardens, huh?" Andrea remarked, as we finally broke through the worst of the traffic. "That's a cute name, you said it was a gated community, right? Aren't those places for, like, rich people and celebrities?"

I shrugged. "Don't get your hopes up, it's probably more like those cheap places for old folks you see in Florida." I couldn't imagine them being able to afford anything better. As far as I was aware in the last few years, they hadn't been doing too hot on the restaurant front. Daniel had been sending them money for a while. He never told me about it, but I saw it in our bank statements. I never mentioned it, though. As far as I was concerned, it was his money and he could do with it what he liked.

"You didn't look it up?" She sounded shocked. "That would've been the first thing I did."

"You didn't look it up after I told you about it," I snapped back.

"Well . . . they're not my in-laws," she said, pouting.

"Trust me, I know their style." I waved my hand dismissively. "It's probably a single story, most likely yellow house, with one bedroom and one bath. They've always been modest, maybe a little kitschy."

"Your father-in-law has great taste in scotch." She glanced at the back seat where we had placed the neatly wrapped bottle and somewhat tacky crockpot, which was adorned with small sunflowers, the theme of their last kitchen. And, I was sure, their new one as well.

"That's the only thing he has great taste in." I said, smirking as I thought about his striped shirts that barely fit over his belly, and the twenty-year-old khaki pants he was always wearing.

"Be nice," she said, chuckling. "I pray that if I ever get married, I have a better relationship with my in-laws."

"*When* you get married," I corrected her. I wasn't someone who believed marriage was the key to happiness, but a husband and kids had always been something Andrea wanted, so I was supportive. "You'll be fine. People like you, remember?"

"People like you, too." Andrea flashed me a crooked smile. "The problem is you don't like people."

"I like you..."

"And Daniel, I hope," she said, laughing.

"Oooh, yeah, him," I stretched out my legs putting my feet on the dash. "He's all right..."

***

As we pulled up to the gate, I kind of . . . no, really couldn't believe my eyes. But there it was, sprawled across the largest, most over the top gate I'd ever seen. *LILITH'S GARDENS*. Written in swirly gold. The ornate detailing on this gate would probably make some people cream their pants, but as someone who knew nothing about architecture, I thought it looked pretty cool.

"So," Andrea let that linger on her lips a bit too long. "It's not exactly what I would call . . . kitschy."

Next to the gate was a nice but small booth made of polished stone. The man inside was large in the muscular kind of way and had a pleasant demeanor. He asked who we were there to see and checked our ID's before letting us in. The gates glided open as we slowly drove up. The long smooth roads were adorned with tall cast-iron street lamps. Every house looked about the same. All made with the same style grey stone, two to three stories, with large sprawling green lawns. Everything looked relatively new. Polished, and incredibly well maintained.

Being that it was relatively dark at this point, I couldn't get a real good look at everything. But the overall style and impression left me speechless. This place looked like it should be in a movie, or some reality TV show about spoiled rich women who spent all day shopping, drinking, and gossiping.

We found what they told us was their home and pulled into their driveway, one so big it could fit six cars with room to spare. The house was two stories, with large windows, and a beautiful stone path lined with short green bushes and flowers that lead from the driveway to the massive oak double front doors.

This couldn't be their house. No way.

"I can't tell you how much I wish there was better lighting." Andrea's face was one of pure awe. "This place is gorgeous. All the pics we could have taken."

"I seriously doubt they're gonna be moving anytime soon," I replied as I stepped out of the car. "We'll get your pics another day."

Andrea grabbed the liquor bottle; I grabbed the crock-pot. As we walked up the path, I tried not to think about how the tacky sunflowers did not match a house like this one. Part of me wanted to trash it. Another part of me knew I couldn't walk in there empty-handed.

Before the bell even finished ringing, the doors flew open. A pair of thin pale arms wrapped around me before I could even mentally process what was happening. Once I was finally released from the overly tight embrace, my eyes widened.

"Lena?" My jaw fell loose, despite myself, as I looked into my mother-in-law's face. This was not the face I was used to, nor the figure.

She had always been a stern-looking woman. Pale as all hell, wrinkled beyond her years, and carrying a bit too much weight. But now, the woman before me was . . . stunning? Her pale skin was tight and surprisingly wrinkle-free. Not so much so that she looked like a young woman, but just enough to look mature, not elderly.

I thought of my own skin. Of the crow's feet that hung around my tired eyes.

Her hair, that was once stringy and dry, now looked fully bodied, healthy, and perfectly curled. And her body – dear God. She went from doughy and soft to a total yoga guru. Her petite figure was perfectly fitted in a classy mauve dress that showed off her bicep muscles.

I thought about my oversized sweater. My old, worn jeans.

"Come in, my dear! It's freezing out there!" She pulled me inside the open marble foyer, which was white and polished to perfection. A large crystal chandelier hung overhead. A large split staircase, straight out of Titanic, led to the floor above. Large windows and glass doors on either side of the double stairs led out to the back, showing off the Olympic-sized pool.

"Your home is amazing," Andrea said, her dark eyes wider than I had ever seen them.

"Thank you, darling," Had she always spoken so clearly? Where was her usual accent? "Here, let me take that for you." Lena took the wrapped bottle from Andrea, then beamed at me warmly. Before this, I honestly had no idea she was capable of smiling. Especially at me. I followed after her, slowly, trying to take the house in. We entered a kitchen that looked like the set of a cooking show. She placed the bottle on the long pristine white kitchen island and gestured for me to put my gift down next to it.

There, a large woman was stirring a pot of what looked like sauce. Honestly. The kitchen smelled incredible. The thick aroma of fresh herbs tickled my nostrils and made my stomach rumble. Lena walked over and extracted three wine glasses; she opened a bottle that had a French name on it that I would never be able to say correctly. With a delicate hand, she poured out the deep ruby liquid then served them to us.

Who was this woman? So refined and pleasant. I saw her... what, six months ago? Was it even possible for someone to change so drastically in such a short time? Disregarding how they would even be able to afford a place like this. Diet, exercise, Botox, maybe a facelift could only get you so far.

"Thank you for having me, Mrs. Kowalski," Andrea said, as she took a sip from her glass. Her eyes sparkled. "Wow, this is delicious."

"Isn't it, just?" the older woman said, chuckling. "And please. Andrea, we've known each other for years, just call me Lena."

"R-right." Andrea looked surprised, Lena usually hardly spoke more than a fragmented sentence to her. Now she was telling her to call her by her first name?

Who the fuck was this woman?

"Why don't we go sit down? Dinner will be ready shortly."

Andrea followed after Lena quickly. I hung back, looking around in disbelief, then emptied my wine glass. Damn, that was delicious. As I poured myself more, I noticed the large woman, presumably their *fucking* private cook, looking at me.

"Don't you tell on me, now." I pointed at her and grinned, her fat face turned pink as she turned back to her cooking.

"Well . . . ain't all this just fine and dandy," I mumbled to myself, as I drank more of the best wine I'd ever had and exited the kitchen.

CHAPTER THREE

Nope . . . Nope. . . Nope. Nope. Nope. Nope.

My mother-in-law's appearance had me speechless, but my father-in-law . . . I was floored. Like Lena, he had lost a considerable amount of weight. The beer belly was no more, and even his jawline appeared to have been chiseled into better shape. His once tobacco-stained teeth were now movie-star white. He was wearing dress pants, not khakis, a crisp button-down, and a sensible suit jacket. He looked ready to attend a garden party where people drank tea and talked about the weather, not like he was about to have dinner with the daughter-in-law he barely tolerated.

"Francis," I said, with an extended hand.

"My dear Riley." His breath smelled like mint instead of cigars and whiskey, like it usually did. I preferred the cigar and whiskey smell, to be honest. "Looks like your glass is almost empty."

He snapped his fingers and a tall man with slicked-back hair appeared with another bottle and poured me more wine. *They had a fucking butler too!* I started looking around for the cameras. *This had to be a prank.*

"Andrea, thank you for coming as well." He took her hand in his, causing her to turn a deep shade of maroon.

"I, um . . ." She cleared her throat. "T-thanks for having me." Andrea usually gave the man googly eyes but this was on a whole other level. I had never seen her so tongue-tied, or so flushed.

"Let's take a seat," Lena said, sitting down herself.

Dinner was amazing. And after my third glass of wine, I found myself relaxing a bit. Not totally off my guard – I still found this situation highly suspect. Maybe I would have been able to move on if their change had just been physical, but hearing them laugh and joke, and even compliment me . . . nope, it didn't add up.

People don't just change like that. Not in six months. Not ever.

There had to be an explanation. I was ashamed of it, and I would never tell anyone I thought so, but the first thing that came to mind was vampires. The artificial charms, the sudden and unexplained glow ups. Perhaps it was my writer's imagination, or the wine in my system. But that idea train ran off the track as soon as we started eating. And as soon as I realized I was being crazy and remembered that vampires weren't real.

Because they weren't . . . right?

"Well, why don't we retire to the lounge?" Francis said, standing up and stepping away from the table. "Have a night-cap before you have to depart."

This from a guy who once belched so forcefully that a little bit of throw up came out.

A small staircase consisting of three steps led down to a luxurious carpet, two long couches, a love seat, and a stone fireplace. Just above the stairs on the tile platform was a grand piano; if either of them started playing, I swear, I would have run for the hills. There was only so much a woman could take.

The butler man came and handed Andrea, Francis, and me glasses of scotch. Lena was given another glass of wine. I noticed Andrea's drink was on the rocks with a twist, which was the way she preferred it. But I didn't think Francis, who had requested the drinks for us, would have known that. I tried to rack my brain for a time he might have seen her drinking scotch, but besides the wedding, there really wasn't one. Could he have remembered? All the way from then?

"I talked to Daniel and he said he will be taking an early flight home," Lena cooed as she nestled into the couch across from me. "He'll come straight here from the airport and should be back no later than tomorrow afternoon. So, I was hoping I could extend your invitation. Why not spend the night? I have some spare pajamas you could wear."

"Oooohh." I felt my throat closing up. "You know I gotta feed Cat . . . "

"I thought she was more of a grazer," she smiled coolly, taking a delicate sip of wine. "Wouldn't she be fine, for just one night?"

"Uh, yeah, I mean. . . " I had left her alone for a whole weekend before, but that wasn't really the issue. "A-Andrea, yeah, Andrea has to get back. She takes her Gram to church every Sunday."

"That's so sweet," Lena purred, her gaze turning to the apparently permanently flushed Andrea. "But I'm sure you wouldn't mind driving back alone? It's not too far, and you haven't had much to drink."

She really hadn't. At dinner she hadn't even touched her glass of wine. *She was too busy drooling over my father-in-law.*

"Y-yeah, I would be fine with that." She looked at me with sorry eyes.

"It's settled then."

Wait, was it? I thought for a moment about arguing but decided against it. Daniel would be here tomorrow. And it was late, I had my fingers crossed they still stuck to their ten o'clock bedtime. They would be out of my hair, and maybe I could snoop around a bit before I hit the hay. I figured a place that big had to have a library. I would have liked nothing better than to curl up with a good book and a glass of whiskey.

But even if they didn't have a library, looking around

the place could be fun.

And maybe I could try and find out how they could have ever in a million fucking years afforded a place like this. But discussing finances in front of a non-family member would have been rude, so I decided to take the cocktail conversation into a different direction.

"You know, as amazing as your new home is," I said with a voice coated in sugar. "I can't get over how fit you two are now! It's amazing, what's your secret?"

"Thank you, Riley dear," Frances chuckled. "But I'm afraid there's no secret; turns out what my doctor had been saying for years was true. I just had to make better food choices and exercise more regularly."

Andrea nodded in agreement. Though part of me wondered if she was actually listening to a word he was saying, or just using conversation as a reason to continue staring at him.

"Well," Lena chimed in. "That's not all. Frances and I have been really into meditation lately. Taking the time to connect to the universe, to all the powers that be. You'd be amazed, Riley, how good that is for the body, and for the soul."

What I wanted to say was, *"So it was meditation, not Botox, that took twenty years off your face?"*

What I actually said was, "That sounds *really* cool." I polished off my drink and was instantly handed another by the butler. That man was becoming my favorite thing about their new place.

"We should try it together sometime." She leaned forward slightly, making scary amounts of eye contact. Didn't she know by now I was an introvert? *How rude!* "Maybe tomorrow morning? Or tonight if you're so inclined."

Well, that was *never* going to happen.

"Maybe," I offered her.

Her small smile remained, but her eyes lost a bit of their shimmer.

***

"You're a traitor," I grumbled as I walked Andrea to her car.

"Look, I'm sorry." I could tell she meant it. And honestly, I wasn't really upset with her, I just wanted to be mad. "It's not all bad, though, right? I mean they were being really nice, way nicer than usual. Maybe you can make this as an opportunity to finally connect with them more? And even if you can't, there are worse places to spend an evening, right? . . . I mean look at it!"

She gestured back to the . . . let's face it . . . mansion.

"But don't you find it weird?" I kept my tone low; they were far away, but for all I knew, they had like superhuman hearing now too. Hell, maybe they could read minds. Anything would make more sense than them just out of nowhere being nice to me.

Well, almost anything. Not the whole vampire thing. That would be silly. *Right?*

"Yes, it's . . . a little weird," Andrea said, nodding. "But you know money changes people. Maybe they were able to sell the restaurant for a lot? Which gave them more time to work on themselves and change their perspective on a few things."

"And get Botox," I said, raising a brow for good measure.

"Well, yeah," she said, chuckling. "Can't really blame them for that . . . and they do look great."

"I don't know, though." I leaned against her car, subtly trying to block her from getting in. "Their place was a hole in the wall. And from what I last heard; it wasn't doing well. How could they have sold it and made enough to afford a place like this?" Andrea shrugged as she reached for the door handle and waited for me to move, which I didn't.

"Why don't you just ask them?" she said, sighing.

"They could lie."

"That's the worst-case scenario," she said, with a smirk on her lips that I wanted to scratch off with my fingernails, then felt guilty for thinking that way. "Best case, you all sit down and have a heart to heart. It's all probably simpler than you think. If anything, I'm sure when Daniel gets here tomorrow, they'll tell him everything. Right?"

"Right." I hated when she was all rational and crap. She smiled at me in such a way that I knew a hug was imminent. And sure enough, her perfect full breasts were squished against my A cups in seconds.

"I'll be home in about forty-five minutes, if you want to talk." She broke the hug, then opened her car door. "Have another drink and try to relax."

She paused before getting into the car, looking at me with her warm brown eyes. “And think about . . . you know . . . trying to connect with them more? It really felt like they were trying tonight. This could be a good opportunity to bond.”

“Yeah, yeah.” I rolled my eyes. “Get going before I jump in there with you.”

I watched her drive away.

I let myself enjoy a moment alone before heading back up the path. No one was in the entranceway, so I assumed my in-laws were still in the "lounge." I walked lazily over to the glass back doors, peered at the large pool. It was lit up and looked so inviting. I leaned against the glass and watched soft wisps of steam rise from its still waters.

"It's lovely, isn't it?" I jumped, Lena was standing inches away from me. How did she sneak up on me like that? I looked at her feet, she was still wearing heels. Was I deaf? Was she secretly Batman? And what was up with my obsession with bat-related things tonight? I needed to chill.

"Does every house in this community have a pool?" I asked, after my heartbeat settled.

"Yes, I believe so." She handed me another drink, which I accepted happily. "You should see Mr. Beelze's pool, twice the size of ours, and he has two Jacuzzi's."

"Who's Mr. Beelze?" *And why did you bring him up out of the blue like that?*

"Dolion Beelze." She clinked her glass against mine, then took a sip before continuing, "He founded this place. In fact, he named this community after his late wife."

"Okay."

"He's a wonderful man. Kind. Generous. This place would truly fall apart without him. He makes everyone who lives here feel like family. I know you would just love him."

Alright. Soooo either she was crushing mad hard on this Dolion fellow, or this was some freaky dicky cult? Or perhaps it was both? Maybe they were all swingers or something. A shiver ran down as I pictured my in-laws swapping keys with a bunch of old, rich white people.

Gross. Though perhaps less now that they were fit and less wrinkled.

"Why don't we rejoin Frances?" I said as I slinked my way around her and dashed off, maybe a bit too quickly, to the "*lounge*."

Or living room,

As normal people called it.

***

Luckily for me, they turned in at ten. Unfortunately for me, I was relatively buzzed and sleepy. Which was super lame and made me feel old, but what could you do? My guest bedroom had its own bathroom. It was a full bath, with a tub and shower. I cleaned up and changed into the silk nightgown that was left out on my bed. It fit me perfectly, and I suspected it was bought with me in mind.

The room was probably about the size of our entire apartment. There was a small bar that had ice chilling, a bottle of Irish whiskey, and a fresh glass next to it. If the room weren't already spinning, I wouldn't have been able to resist. But in my state, all I could manage was fumbling over to the balcony.

Yes, the room had its own view. But at that point, I felt no shock.

I lit a cigarette and took in the view. Their backyard was killer. Next to the pool was a sleek bar, fully stocked and illuminated with warm light. A bit past the pool was a gazebo with a large grill and a few tables. You could throw a real rager in a yard like that – I feared it would go to waste in my in-law's hands. But who knew? They weren't the same stuck up, cold people I was used to. Maybe they did party now.

"Key parties," I chuckled to myself as I finished my smoke. As I headed back inside, I felt a bit more sober so I contemplated making another drink. But then . . . *Bang!* Just outside my door. It sounded like something heavy had fallen. My first thought was that it might have been a person. I rushed to the door and opened it.

"Hello?" The hallway was dark. And without the foggiest idea where the light switch was, I ventured out with my phone light on. "Everything okay?"

I walked toward where I thought the sound had come from. My in-laws were on the other side of the split staircase, but maybe it was the butler or chef? I worried about it being the chef, she had been rather large. If she had fallen, I wasn't one hundred percent sure I could lift her on my own.

"Hello??" I called out a little louder this time.

Nothing.

I was about to turn back when I saw a flicker of movement at the end of the corridor. I squinted. Pointing my phone light in the general direction, I saw where the movement came from and stepped closer. As I walked, I felt the air around me turning colder. When I neared the end of the hall, even my breath was visible. Movement again. Coming from the room at the end of the hall. The door was open, but it was pitch black inside. I was nearly there when something within me told me not to take another step.

That was when I finally spotted it, long and dark, moving up the door frame. At first, I thought it was a spider. A large one. But as I shined my light on it, I saw nails. Fingernails. It was a . . . hand?

Nope.

I took a step back. *Perhaps I wasn't quite as sober as I'd thought.*

The hand moved, finger by finger up the door frame. Slowly. The hand's flesh was pitch black. A dark substance dripped down the skin as it moved. Every breath seemed to have escaped my throat. I wanted to shout for help. But I felt like no words could form, like I was suddenly mute.

From the darkness within the room, I saw something stirring. Just as slowly as the hand had moved, if not slower. It emerged: long, dark strings spanning almost the entire length of the door. It looked like . . . like hair?

Nope.

I stepped back even further. Within the wild mess of tangles, I saw a face appear, just as black as the hand's flesh, and dripping. It was a dark mass, barely distinguishable from its hair, except for its eyes. Wide and bloodshot, the pupils dilated until the irises were as black as the night sky. A long dark leg emerged from the door, stepping onto the floor, a puddle of liquid spilling below its foot.

Nope!

I turned around and ran.

Nope!

Down the staircase.

Nope!

Out the front door.

Nope!

As fast as my scrawny legs could carry me.

CHAPTER FOUR

What Do I Do If I Don't Believe In Anything?

My bare feet pounded against the pavement. My heart was up in my throat and my mind wouldn't stop racing. Trying to gather some semblance of what I had just witnessed. I didn't believe in ghosts. I didn't. But that . . . that wasn't human. So what did that leave me with? If I were the protagonist in a horror novel . . . what would be my next move? Usually the first ghost's or whatever's appearance was followed by the protagonist either passing out or running back to their room and telling themselves they had dreamed the whole thing. Well . . . as much as I wasn't one to shy away from living in denial, there was also no way I was going back into that house, not with that thing in there!

So what would the protagonist do after they accepted their situation and decided to deal with it? Go to a church?

Get a priest? I grimaced at the thought. But my only other option besides that would be to find a psychic, and that seemed even less favorable. I had only had my palm read once, and that lady had been full of shit. So I opened my phone, still in a full sprint, and did a quick search.

There was a church nearby. Now I just needed a ride. I opened my app and saw there was a driver five minutes away, so I plugged in the church's address. I reached the gate and hit the button that lets you out.

"Miss, are you okay?!" As I ran past the gate, the security guard yelled after me.

But I didn't stop, running in the direction that the driver was coming. Half a block down, I saw him, waving my arms like a maniac. It was a miracle he stopped. I flung the back door open and hopped in.

"You're . . . you're . . . Riley, right?" He appeared to be slightly nervous.

I must have seemed crazy.

"Yes! So, drive, like now, man! Now!"

"Okay, okay." Now he just sounded annoyed. "You don't have to yell. Now I see why you have such a low rating."

Even as he drove away, my heart wouldn't settle. Its pulse was so strong, I felt it would burst out of my chest. I closed my eyes and tried to relax my breathing. What I saw back there, I needed to get it out of my head. It was too much – I felt like I was going insane. To distract myself, I started counting backward from one hundred, but gave up on that quickly. Numbers were never my forte. Next, I went to a nursery rhyme. I started with a little *Baa Baa Black Sheep.* But sheep have always freaked me out. They're honestly just fluffy goats. And goats are just evil. Everyone knows that.

So, I went to *Twinkle, Twinkle Little Star*. Then I started wondering if both bloody rhymes had the same tune. So, I started going line by line. And . . . what a jip - they totally were. Was this something people knew? Did I just discover something? Or did everyone already know this, and I was just an idiot?

"Miss," the driver rudely interrupted my train of thought and brought me back to my horrible situation.

I might have started glaring at him. I might not have.

"We're here," he sighed, then started taking off his jacket.

"Stripping won't make me rate you any higher, you know," I said, crinkling my nose. "And unless you've got a six-pack under there, which I doubt, it might even make me give you fewer stars."

"I'm not stripping," he snapped, throwing his jacket at me. "It's winter and you're wearing a fucking silk slip."

"Right." As I slipped on the jacket, I got slapped in the face with Old Spice, used to cover up the underlining skunk of Mary Jane. "Thanks."

I peered out of the window at the small brick church. It looked dark, and a bit tacky, to be honest. I glanced at the time on my phone. It would be a few hours before anyone would show up, but I wasn't going back to that house. No way. And I didn't have my wallet, so a motel was out. So, I breathed in and opened the door. Before leaving, I turned to the driver.

"Even with the jacket, I'm only giving you two stars. You drive like a grandma."

I saw him flip me off as I slammed the door.

As he drove away, I gave him the two stars, but tipped him ten bucks . . . for the jacket.

***

"Hey." Someone touched my shoulder, "Miss?"

I swatted the hand away.

"Excuse me, miss, if you need help, I can call someone. But I can't let you sleep here."

I opened my eyes, part of me expecting to see Daniel's bright baby blues. But instead, I was greeted by deep almond-shaped eyes, the kind of eyes you could just sink into. I looked around, taking in my surroundings. I must have fallen asleep on the church's front step. The events from last night spilled back into my consciousness, I felt my eyes watering up.

"You have to help me," I reached out and grabbed the man's arm, that's when I noticed the stiff white collar around his neck. "You're a priest, right? I got a situation that I think totally calls for one of you guys."

"Miss, I . . . can call someone for you." He tried to move his arm away from me, but I held onto that thing harder than a puppy who's got its teeth in its favorite chew toy.

"No, I don't need someone!" I stood, my grip on him unrelenting, "I need you! A priest person! There's something freaky going on at my in-law's house."

"I think what you're looking for is a family counselor." He raised his thick dark eyebrows at me in a sassy kind of way that even someone like me, who had never been in the same room as a priest, knew he probably shouldn't have. It wasn't very Godly of him, for sure.

"No, it's not like my in-laws are being freaky. Well, I mean . . . they kind-of are. But that could just be because they've got money now. Rich people are usually weird, right? Like Tom Cruise." His sassy expression somehow grew sassier the more I talked. "Last night I saw some straight-up *Ring* girl shit and I'm not having it, man. Full disclosure, I never believed in any of this stuff. And I've got no idea what the fuck is going on. All I know is that I'm not gonna be that dumb white bitch in the movie that dismisses shit till she gets possessed or something."

"So, you want me to come to your in-law's house and bless it?" he asked in such a nonchalant way that it really pissed me off.

"I don't know! I just want you to do whatever it is that you people do to get rid of ghosts!"

"Look, miss," he said, finally breaking out of my grasp.

"You're not a member of this church, and I'm not a ghost-buster. Are you even Catholic?"

"Well, no." I felt a pit forming in my stomach. Was this guy really not going to help me? "I can join your church if I have to. I mean now that I saw a ghost . . . who knows?"

"You can't just join. This isn't like a gym membership. And besides, you wouldn't understand our services here."

"I'm not, like, inept or anything." I said, suddenly feeling the heat rising in my face. Don't yell at the priest you're trying to get to help you, Riley . . . don't do it.

"Do you speak Vietnamese?" he said, smirking. "We're a Vietnamese congregation. Couldn't you tell by the sign?"

He tilted his head over toward the large board that had the church's name. Saint something I couldn't pronounce. And underneath was a bunch of letters making up words I couldn't read.

"I thought that was like, Latin, or something."

"Right." His tone conveyed the eye roll he suppressed.

Was he the sassiest priest in the world, or had TV and movies just painted this false pretense of priestly virtue?

"Service is going to begin shortly," he continued. "So, miss, I would really appreciate it if you left. I can call you a cab."

"I have my own phone, thanks," I knew I was pouting like a child at this point, but I couldn't help it. My whole world had been flipped upside down. I liked it better when ghosts lived inside books or television screens. When I could sit back with a beer and popcorn and laugh at the silly idiots as they followed a strange sound down into their basement. I had even preferred it when my in-laws were poor and judgmental. How had I gotten myself into this mess?

"It still has power?"

I lifted it up to my face, pressed the button, but the screen stayed black... "No."

"Alright," he sighed. "Come in for a second, you can use my office phone."

He unlocked the front doors and we walked inside. Only when I entered, did I realize just how chilled to the bone I was. My teeth started chattering. And for the first time, I saw some concern on the sassy priest's face.

"What's your name?" he asked, as he led me past the lobby into a small room with an even smaller desk and a couch that looked lumpy.

"What do you care?" I crossed my arms in defiance. "Why even bother asking?"

"Look, I might not be able to help you with ... how do you put it ... your freaky *Ring* girl situation." He sat down behind the desk in a chair that was most likely from a discount store, then gestured to me to sit in one of the two seats across from him. As I sat, the hard chair beneath me squeaked something awful. "But that doesn't mean we can't be civil, right? I'm Father Lanh."

"Like, Lamb?" I looked at him for a beat.

"No . . . Lanh,"

"L . . . Lain?"

"Lanh, " he said, a bit slower.

"L-Land?"

"Where'd the D come from?" The corner of his lips lifted a bit, almost forming a smile.

"Urgh, sorry, umm," I felt heat rushing to my face. "L-lawn?"

"Close enough." He chuckled as he pushed a chunky green landline over toward me. I didn't even know people still had landlines. I looked at it, imagining myself picking it up. Calling my mother-in-law, going back there. To where that *thing* was.

"Look, ummm . . . Lawn . . . Father person. I can't go back there, not without you. That thing was, like, coming at me. Like it was going to eat me or possess me or whatever ghostly things like to do. I mean, I don't live there. But my in-laws do. What if . . . whatever that thing was gets them? I'm like eighty percent sure my in-laws are Catholic so . . . can't you help some God-fearing folks like them?"

He leaned back in his seat, studying my face. I took the opportunity to get a good look at him too. He was relatively young. I would guess my age. Maybe a bit younger. He had a nice golden tan. And if his hair weren't so short, he was closing in on skin-head territory, I'd even venture to say he'd be kind of attractive.

"My name's Riley . . . by the way."

"Okay, Riley." He stood up. "Wait here a moment, I'll get Father Tran to cover for today's sermon."

"You're actually going to help me?" I couldn't believe it . . . what had convinced him exactly? My embarrassingly bad pronunciation of his name? My raving about ghosts? Or maybe it was the oversized jacket that smelled like weed and the no shoes that screamed *help this lady*.

"If my coming and blessing the house could give you peace of mind, and help your in-laws feel safer, I don't see the harm. Though, this is unorthodox."

"Don't you mean Orthodox?" It was a stupid joke, but now that I knew he was going to help, I felt so much more relaxed.

He looked like he was going to say something else but at the last minute decided against it and settled for a small shake of the head. "I'll be right back."

***

"Your in-laws live here?" He raised a questioning brow at me as we pulled up to the security gate. "I was expecting an old Victorian, not some multi-million-dollar mansion."

"They're mini-mansions, at best," I said, as I showed the security guy my ID. I was relieved he wasn't the same guy as last night. That guy probably thought I was a lunatic and who knew if he'd let me back in. "Maybe the ghost or whatever is a classy bitch. No rickety old houses for her. She moves into the new ones."

"Well, I suppose homes this large would have a lot of unused rooms," he remarked, as he drove past the gate.

"Is that how this freaky stuff works? Dead souls or whatever just wander into empty rooms?"

"I can't say for sure. That's just something my grandmother told me."

“Your grandmother? Didn't they teach you this stuff in, like, exorcism class or whatever, when you went to priest school?"

"Nope. No exorcism class at priest school."

"That really sucks." I sank lower into my seat, as we approached the house. "So what are you gonna do, exactly, to get rid of that thing?"

"I'll go room to room and bless them, say a quick prayer in each. Splash a little holy water."

"That's it?" I was starting to feel skeptical.

"That's it." He pulled into their driveway. "Am I at the right . . . mini-mansion?"

“Yeah,” I nodded. "Will that work?"

"Try not to worry, Riley." He placed his hand on my shoulder. It was warm. "What you saw might not have been something bad or malicious. And if it was the soul of someone who has passed, I promise you, they can do you no harm."

"You're sure?"

“Positive. If it helps I actually did learn that in priest school. Are you ready to go inside?"

“Ready as I'll ever be.” I took a deep breath and opened the car door.

***

"Riley!" Lena's boney arms wrapped around me tightly, "Oh, I was so worried! Daniel will be here in two hours! I had no idea how to tell him we lost his wife!"

I waited there with limp arms, for the embrace to end.

"Sorry, Lena," I grumbled.

"Who's this?" she asked, finally letting me go.

"That's Lawn." I stepped aside so they could introduce themselves to one another.

"Father Lanh, actually," he said, as he and Lena shook hands. "Riley wanted me to bless your new home."

"Really?" Lena looked at me with confusion plastered across her face. "Daniel always told me you hated anything and everything that had to do with religion."

Lawn shot a small smirk in my direction.

"That's a bit of an exaggeration," I huffed. Sure, I'd always considered myself an atheist, but I wasn't like, hateful, toward other people's beliefs. I just thought it was all kind of dumb. Part of me, even after what I saw, felt stupid for bringing a priest here.

In fact, the events from last night almost felt like a dream. *Almost*. Lena invited us inside, but as I went to pass her, she grabbed my arm and pulled me close to her.

"You know we have our own congregation, right? We could have brought our priest over to bless the house."

"Yeah... but does that matter? A priest's a priest, right?"

She frowned, as I wiggled my arm out of her grasp.

I turned to Lawn with a forced smile. "Welcome to their *humble* home."

***

The whole thing took about an hour. Their place had way too many rooms. There was one room that literally just had art in it! *What the heck was that shit for?* When we reached the room the *Ring* lady came out of, I asked Lawn to do it twice. He complied, again looking like he might have wanted to crack a joke or tease me, but at the last-minute showed restraint. Weren't priests, like, supposed to be uptight and boring? Because I had a feeling that Lawn wasn't.

My father-in-law was MIA for all of this. When I asked Lena, she said he had an important meeting to attend. Which I thought was weird, considering it was Sunday morning. But hey, what wasn't weird? If someone told me yesterday I'd be standing in a haunted mansion with a priest, wine would have squirted out of my nostrils . . .

That's how much I would have laughed.

Lena dismissed herself before we were even halfway finished, saying she needed to meditate. When every room was all good and blessed, and hopefully ghost-free, I walked Lawn to his car. I'd been relatively silent during the last half hour or so, just watching him do his thing. I couldn't shake the feeling that I had overreacted in bringing him here.

But then I would remember those black, blood-shot eyes.

"Do you feel better now?" he asked with sincerity in his tone. "I know this isn't really what you believe, but I hope it gave you some solace."

I didn't like it when he was being all nice. I much preferred the sass.

"So, do I like . . . tip you?"

He let out a snort.

"If you feel like you owe me something, why don't you donate to a charity? That can be my payment." He got in the car. But before shutting the door, he looked at me once more. "And it doesn't have to be a religious charity, just donate to a cause you believe in."

“And . . . what do I do if I don't believe in anything?” I flashed him a crooked smile.

“We all have something we believe in.” There was a soft twinkle in his eye. “Or at the very least, someone.”

I gave him a look that made him chuckle.

“Goodbye Riley, it was . . . interesting meeting you.”

I watched him drive away, then turned back to the house, not really feeling any better.

But not any worse either.

CHAPTER FIVE

Meditation Room . . . Hmm?

"You really brought a priest to my parents' house?" Daniel looked at me in disbelief, and I didn't blame him after all the times I had refused to even step foot in any house of worship. Just another thing that really pissed his parents off when we were getting married. I honestly surprised myself that my first thought was to get to a church. But if I had learned anything from the endless hours I spent reading R.L. Stein and Stephen King growing up, it was that if something freaky and supernatural was after you, it was way better to at least try and get help. And also, that cops were useless in these situations, hence why I had opted for a priest. But I wasn't going to explain all of that to Daniel.

He hadn't seen what I had. Shit like that changes people. Not that I was about to become a regular church-goer or anything. People don't change *that* much.

"I felt some bad juju in here." I decided not to mention the *Ring* girl. I was hopeful that Lawn's magic water did what it was supposed to, and the house was now ghost-free, so why make myself sound crazy?

Well . . . crazier.

"So bad that you ran out of here in the middle of the night?" His eyes searched my face for an explanation.

"How about we drop it, yeah?" Was all I offered in return.

"Riley, come on," he said, with a smirk.. "Were you spooked being in such a large house? I told you watching scary movies all the time would make you paranoid."

"Speaking of large houses," I said, ignoring his question, as well as his rude comment about my love of horror cinema. "What do you think of your parent's new shindigs?"

"It's definitely something," he remarked, looking around the guest room with wide eyes. "This one room might be the size of our apartment."

Nah, it's probably bigger.

"And your parents, they look . . . different."

"Yeah, it's great seeing them looking so healthy," he smiled way too proudly. "Mother told me they started meditating and eating better a while back."

"Yeah . . ." I wondered if questioning his parent's sudden transformation would tick one of his buttons, so I decided to hold that off for later. After all, I had a feeling he wasn't super happy with me, as there was something odd about his vibe. I couldn't really figure it out, but his eyes just seemed . . . different. "So did you know they were going to get such a . . . large home?"

"Not really," he shrugged. "I mean, before booking my flight back, I did look this gated community up. I was . . . surprised. But from everything I've read, it's a great place to live."

"But how. . . " *The fuck could they afford this place?* Was what I wanted to say, but I decided to rephrase that, "So why did they decide to move here, specifically?"

"Well," Daniel sat on the bed's edge, and indicated for me to do the same. "The guy that runs this place, Dolion Beelze, he was the one that bought their restaurant."

"Really?" I did as he wanted and sat down next to him, though honestly, I would have preferred going out onto the balcony for a smoke.

"And during the whole process, they became friendly. He was the one that got them into meditating, eating better, and eventually, he told them that his community here had a vacancy."

"So, he bought their restaurant, then essentially got his money back by letting them buy this place?" What a hustler.

Respect.

"You would see it that way," he said, nudging me playfully.

I felt mildly satisfied with that explanation, though

the whole thing was still fucking weird.

"So, when do you want to head back home?" Even if I knew how they got this place, that didn't mean I wanted to stay. Even if Lawn did get rid of the *Ring* girl, and honestly to me, that was a big if, my whole belief system was rattled and I kind of wanted to go home and cuddle with my cat.

"About that," he said, flashing me big puppy eyes that basically told me I wasn't going to like the rest of this conversation. "The community here is having a welcoming party for my parents tonight, and they really want us to stay."

Yep . . . Didn't like what he said one bit.

"Well . . . tomorrow's Monday, you know?" I stood from the bed and walked over to the balcony. Daniel followed a few steps after me. Once outside, I lit a cigarette and took a drag as I gazed out onto their amazing backyard. It looked even better in the daylight, which kind of pissed me off a bit.

"I don't have to go into the office till Wednesday." He took a cig from my pack for himself. "Mother said she has a spare laptop you can use for work. And if you're worried about Cat, I texted Andrea and she said she wouldn't mind feeding her."

This all seemed so well thought out, for something he claimed was a spur of the moment. I found it hard to believe he didn't know his parents were moving here, that they just so happened to move in when he was away, how he was able to get a flight back so quickly. And now there was a party that his parents didn't mention yesterday and everything was all perfectly set up so that I really had no reason to refuse to stay one or two more nights. Why all the secrecy?

I took a long drag. "I have nothing to wear."

He wrapped his arm around my waist and pulled me closer.

"Mother has a few dresses that will fit you." He rested his cheek against the top of my head. "And if you don't like any of them, we can go and buy you something."

"Alright." I sighed. I could have fought harder, but I felt there was no point. He kissed my forehead and smiled at me, but his eyes looked a bit distant. Or maybe I just felt distant. *Off.* I didn't want to stay in that house, butI didn't want to tell him why. But I figured, at least tonight, I wouldn't be alone. And if *Ring* girl came at me again . . . I could just throw Daniel at her and book it out of there . . .

That was a comforting thought.

***

So there I was, standing in front of the largest house I'd ever seen. We are talking castle status. It was less modern but had a similar design to the rest of the homes here. Though it was jacked up to the ninth degree. It looked to be four or five stories, with a wide tower-looking thing at the center . . . I'm not an architect . . . I don't know the correct term. But I could totally picture a princess being locked up in there. But again, perhaps that was my writer's mind taking over.

You could fit five regular-sized houses on the sprawling jade green front lawn. I felt bad for whoever's job it was to maintain the landscape around here. This lawn and all its hedges and perfectly trimmed trees probably took a week of maintenance alone.

It was all so . . . unreal.

I should have taken a shot before we left for the party, or maybe two or three.

At the front door, there were two butlers dressed in tuxes taking people's coats. Past them, another two dudes were passing out champagne. It was all very *Great Gatsby.* I accepted the beverage with a small smile, though I really wanted something stronger . . . I would have taken what I could get.

I looked over at Daniel and his parents. They seemed to blend in with this crowd perfectly. Daniel had always been tall and fit and seemed to just be getting better looking with age. Even I was amazed at how well he looked in a tailored suit, with his blonde locks slicked back neatly. And now with his parents all prim and proper, they looked like a real posh family. But me? I felt totally out of my element. That black floor-length dress probably cost more than I made in a month and hugged my body so well, it gave off the illusion that I had curves. Yet even with that dress, I felt like I looked like a complete ragamuffin next to them.

We walked into a freaking ballroom! The walls and floor were made of white marble. The floor was so polished, everything reflected in it like it was still water. The walls were lined on all sides with large intricately designed windows. Directly across from the entrance to the ballroom were massive double doors made of glass that led out into the mansion's backyard. The room was illuminated by a chandelier that looked bigger than the house where I grew up in Jersey, as well as modern lights that lined the room's ceiling. The place was filled with smiling, laughing, beautiful people, with teeth so white I wish I had shades. Ages varied but everyone looked healthy, wealthy, and way more put together than I could or would ever hope to be. I noticed a bar a short distance away and downed my glass of champagne.

It just wasn't cutting it.

Daniel followed me to the bar, and it was only then I noticed his own glass was finished, and he looked a bit tense. He placed his hand on the small of my back and ordered us two whiskeys. His parents were near and talking to a young blonde woman who had a body straight out of Playboy, but the style and grace of Scarlett O'Hara.

"Hey." I nudged Daniel lightly in his rib cage. "You okay?"

"This is just . . ." He looked around, then looked at me with a cocked brow. "I mean . . . this is kind of a lot, right?"

"Thank God!" I chuckled, letting my body lean into his slightly. "I didn't want to be rude or anything but this place is like . . . a movie set!"

"It's a bit over the top, for sure." He laughed, as his hand glided from the small of my back to my hip, drawing me in closer. "Sorry if I seemed off earlier. To be honest, this whole thing has been like a whirlwind."

"Tell me about it." I clinked my glass against his and we both drank.

"Thank you for being so cool about all this . . . Well, except for the priest thing," he said, and laughed. "Are you ever going to tell me what that was all about?"

Before I could say anything, Daniel's parents came over to us with the hot blonde. I found myself in awe of how her long locks shimmered in the chandelier's lights, knowing full well my bleached and overly dry hair probably looked like straw compared to hers.

"Daniel, Riley, we'd like you to meet our neighbor, Erica."

"Nice to meet you." Daniel politely extended his hand, but his gesture was ignored as she jumped in and enveloped him in a way-too-friendly embrace.

Fuck . . . a hugger.

Knowing I was likely to be her next victim, I tried to look for a way out. But her greeting came sooner than I expected, and with little warning, she had me in a bear hug I wished I could have tapped out of. She smelled like roses and her perky tits were real, much to my chagrin. She pulled away, her bright blue eyes looking at me with what seemed to be actual excitement.

"It's so wonderful to meet you all!" Her dainty hands were firmly grasped onto mine. I couldn't get over how soft and flawless her skin was. She had a wedding ring on her finger, so I assumed she had to be at least in her twenties. But

If I had to venture a guess, I'd say she was just barely twenty. "Lena and Frances told me so much about you guys."

"How? They moved in, like, yesterday?" I saw Daniel shaking his head slightly. I reminded myself that I needed to play nice but Malibu Barbie was making it tough. Not only was she holding my hands, but she was also preventing me from taking a sip of my drink. Furthermore, if she made me spill it, there would be hell to pay. I didn't care that it was an open bar. *Nobody wasted whiskey.*

"Well, my hubby and I helped them unpack." She grinned even wider, still not letting go of my hands. I struggled with the urge to yank them away. "Speaking of my darling hubby, let me call him over, so you can meet!"

She turned around, finally letting go. I quickly took another sip as I watched her drag over a man, who, keeping in theme with this party, was a total hunk. Almost Daniel's height, maybe half an inch taller. He had a creamy olive complexion, with large honey brown eyes and dark wavy locks of hair that neatly lined his face. The only thing that wasn't completely perfect about him was his nose, which was a bit large for his face and had a slightly bent ridge like it might have been broken once years ago. But I kind of liked it, as it added some character to his features.

"This is my hubby." She was practically radiating excitement.

"My name's Thomas, but people usually call me Tom," he greeted us with a warm smile and no hug, making me like him a bit more than his wife.

"Except me!" she exclaimed, leaning up to kiss him on the cheek. "He's my sweet Tommy."

Yuck.

"I'm Daniel," Daniel smiled, then gestured to me. "This is my wife, Riley."

"It's great to finally meet you. We've heard so much about you."

I fought the eye roll. *I really did.* But it must have slipped out a bit because I saw a slight frown forming on Daniel's lips.

"It's nice to meet you both," I said quickly, as I took another sip from my almost empty glass.

"We're really happy to have such wonderful neighbors," Thomas said, as he held up four fingers in the bartender's direction. "We just moved in ourselves and were a bit nervous until we met Lena and Frances."

"Oh, stop," Lena said waving her hand. "Aren't they just so sweet!"

I really wanted to get out of this little love fest.

"Daniel, you're really lucky to have such cool parents," the blonde bombshell giggled. "I just might try to steal them."

Everyone laughed.

Except me.

I finished my drink.

Thomas walked past me to the bar, taking my empty glass from my hand, flashing me a sly wink then quickly replaced my beverage. The color of the whiskey he handed me was richer than the one I had previously. He handed a glass to Daniel, and another to Frances, keeping the last for himself.

"It's Macallan, twenty-five years. Have you had it?" He was looking at me when he asked the question, so I shook my head in response. "Really? Frances told me you were a woman who enjoyed her whiskey, so I'm surprised."

"She's more of an Irish whiskey gal." Frances smiled at me, but I wasn't too fond of his tone.

"She's always liked the large, cheaper bottles," Daniel said, laughing.

Thanks Daniel.

"I understand that it's good to enjoy the classics." Thomas winked at me again; one more time and I'd glue the damn thing shut. "But every now and again, one should experience the finer things in life, don't you agree?"

I responded by looking him up and down.

"Well, cheers," Frances interrupted my glare and held up his glass. "To new beginnings,"

Lena and the Marilyn Monroe doppelganger held up their champagne glasses, and the men did the same with their whiskey. I hesitated for a second, till I saw the look in Daniel's eye. After everyone clinked glasses and I took a sip of the best whiskey I'd ever tasted, I knew I had to get out of this weird circle jerk.

"Excuse me," I said with a fake yet polite smile. "I'm just going to step outside for a smoke."

"Now?" Daniel said in a way that meant, *not now.*

"Do you mind if I join you?" Thomas interjected. "I never can fully enjoy whiskey without a smoke, I'm afraid."

I wanted to say no.

But Daniel was annoyed enough as it was, and I knew I would just have been digging myself a deeper grave if I refused. "Suuuuuurrree."

***

The backyard was even more lavish and over the top than the ballroom. There wasn't one, but *two* hedge mazes. Not to mention an enormous pool, the aforementioned Jacuzzis, two outdoor bars, and the whole place was decorated with these crazy flower arrangements in elegant planters made of marble that reached my height.

I let out a heavy breath as I lit my cigarette.

"A bit much, isn't it?" Thomas chuckled; his velvety eyes seemed to be watching me carefully, which was a little unsettling.

"You moved here," I said with a cocked brow.

"It was my wife's idea, believe it or not." He lit his own

cigarette with a lighter engraved with what looked to be diamonds in the shape of a T . . . yeah, he belonged here.

"So, you hate it here?" That time I let the eye roll happen.

"Well, it's better than where I was before." He took a long drag, looking out into the garden. His eyes seemed to darken slightly, but then he turned his attention back to me with a cool smile. "You and Daniel live in Manhattan, right? I've always loved cities. Being able to stay out until the wee hours of the morning. All the lights. The noise. The smells . . ."

"Trust me, man," I said, smirking. "The smells get old real fast."

"So, will you and Daniel be moving here?" It was weird to hear someone ask such a weighted question so lightly.

"What? No . . . no. We love where we are. Why would you ask that? Did his parents say something?"

"No, no," he said, with a chuckle. "It's just such a large house, and Daniel's parents are older, I guess I assumed that might be the plan."

"Well, it's not." I took a heavy drink. At the very least it better not be. Until that point, the idea hadn't even occurred to me. But this Thomas dude was right. It was a big house, outside the city, in a gated community. A perfect place to start a family . . . but then there was the *Ring* girl problem . . .

"Thomas," I said, after taking another drag.

"Like I said before, you can call me Tom," he interrupted me with a smooth grin.

“No, that's okay,” I retorted, before getting back to what I wanted to say. "How long have you and your wife been here?"

"We arrived right after our honeymoon. So, about a week and a half now."

"Didn't realize you were newlyweds," I said flatly. "So, uh, congrats or whatever."

"Thank you . . . or whatever." He seemed oddly amused, and I didn't much care for the way he was looking at me. Even when we were with everyone else, especially when Daniel was standing right there. This guy's eyes never seemed to leave me for long. It was then that he kind-of started to inch closer to me as we talked. This guy was a smooth operator. I needed to be on my guard.

"Anyway, have either of you seen anything like . . . weird or otherworldly around here?" I took a small step back.

"What do you mean?” He moved closer to me, more brazen than before.

"Well . . ." I took another small step back. "Like . . . maybe something spooky? Think Japanese horror movies from the late nineties."

"Sorry." His smile was broad and slightly crooked. He stepped even closer, I went to step back and found myself against a wall. *A wall?* Fucking seriously? How did I manage to get my back pressed against a wall in a yard this fucking big? “I'm not much of a horror fan."

"S'okay," I mumbled, as I tried desperately not to look into his eyes. "Forget I said anything."

He chuckled as he sipped his drink, then leaned in till his lips were right next to my ear.

"But I'll be sure to keep my eyes out for anything *weird* or *otherworldly.*"

I hated his cool, low voice. I hated his smirk. I took a looooooong drag and blew the smoke in his face.

"Thanks," I moved to the left, sliding past him.

I started to walk back inside when he called out, "Riley,"

I thought about ignoring him and rejoining the party. I really did. But despite my annoyance, I turned back. And when I did, his smile grew twofold.

"I like you.”

"The feeling’s not really mutual." I grumbled, which he clearly found funny as he released a short laugh.

"I'm going to give you a piece of advice." Thomas slowly walked toward me.

"Because you like me so much?" Those words were followed by an overly dramatic eye roll.

"Exactly. Keep your distance from the guy that runs this place."

"Umm, okay . . ."

"And whatever you do, don't go into the meditation room." He let his cigarette fall to the ground and stubbed it out with his polished shoe.

"Meditation room?" I raised my brow.

"Yes, the meditation room." He leaned in closer to me again. "No matter what anyone says, no matter what they tell you. Never, under any circumstances, enter the meditation room."

He placed his hand on my shoulder firmly, and his eyes studied my face intently, like he was looking for something. His hand was large and warm, but unwelcome. I was about to tell him to let go, but he beat me to the punch and tucked his hand into his pocket.

"You don't have to like me, Riley," he said as he walked back toward the ballroom. "But it would be in your best interests to follow my advice."

I stood there watching him walk away lazily. Before entering the ballroom, he turned to me once more, sending another one of his stupid winks my way. *Asshole . . .*

I looked up at the massive mansion, at the tall tower at its center.

"Meditation room . . . hmm?" I mumbled to myself, before heading back inside.

CHAPTER SIX

Devour Me

Once inside, I beelined straight for Daniel. He was still by the bar, but his parents were working their way around the room, mingling with others. The bombastic blonde was gone as well. Instead, I found Daniel talking to the definition of a silver fox dressed in a light grey tailored suit that did him many favors. His pepper hair was slicked back just enough to be appropriate for a party like this, but not so much as to be stuffy. He had a full mustache that I normally wouldn't like. I was always under the opinion that mustaches were the rugs of the face, and I was more of a hardwood floor type gal. But on him, I couldn't really find fault with it.

"Riley!" Daniel waved me over, the light was back in his eyes. He looked about ten times more comfortable than he had before I left. "Riley, this is Mr. Beelze. Mr. Beelze, this is my wife, Riley."

"Riley." His voice was as smooth as his looks; he extended his hand and I accepted it without a second thought. Only then did I hear Thomas' warning play in the back of my mind. *Stay away from the guy who runs this place . . .* "We're so happy you both could join us to celebrate Frances and Lena joining our little community."

"We're the ones who should be thanking you," Daniel said, throwing an arm around me. "For throwing my parents such a warm welcome."

"Your home is amazing," I blurted out, not following the flow of conversation at all. I suddenly felt my nerves rising. It wasn't like I trusted Thomas or really believed him. Yet I couldn't shake the feeling that this was all really strange. And it wasn't just that Daniel's parents suddenly got rich, it wasn't even the whole scary *Ring* girl thing, it was the whole vibe of this place that disturbed me. And no matter how much I enjoyed looking at him, this Mr. Beelze was at the center of everything.

"That's very kind of you to say, Riley." His cool blue eyes dug into my own in a way that made me both scared . . . and a little turned on. "This community was mine and my late wife's dream. It took many years of planning, but I must admit, I am truly pleased with the final result. I just wish my wife could have seen it."

"I'm so sorry," Daniel said appropriately, while I just stared at this *fine ass* man trying to fight back drool. Wondering why the fact that he built all this for his deceased wife was somehow checking a box that I didn't know I had.

He held up his hand eloquently. "It was a long time ago." He tilted his head slightly; a soft smile crossed his delicious lips. "I hope you both are enjoying yourselves tonight. Frances and Lena told everyone about the two of you. I have to say, we were all so excited you could be here."

Again. How in the world did they have time to tell everyone about us? How was everyone so chummy, so quickly? I knew Daniel's parents had changed a lot, but they were never friendly people. They never seemed to have many friends, as far as I could tell. And it had always seemed like they preferred to keep to themselves, aside from the restaurant.

Heck. They weren't even nice to their regulars back then.

Also, why was this guy turning me on so much? I felt seriously flushed. Every word that came out of his mouth sounded like music to me. I felt my eyes keep going to that stupidly perfect mustache. I was mesmerized by the bloody thing. Which was absurd – I hated facial hair! *Snap out of it, Riley!*

Your husband is literally right here, I told myself. *Arm around you and everything.*

"Well, we're excited to be here." Daniel replied, pleasantly. "And I can't tell you how happy I am that my parents moved here. I feel like they are much safer here than where they were before."

"Yeah, gated communities are great." I was scraping at the bottom of the barrel. But I knew I couldn't not talk. That would be weird . . . that being said, I sounded like a bumbling idiot.

"Indeed, they are." His eyes still locked onto mine, his smile seemed a little more devilish. I wondered if he could tell how much he was making me flustered, or if this was all happening in my head. "Now, if you will excuse me, I'm afraid I must mingle."

Daniel and Mr. Beelze nodded at one another as he departed. I turned to the bar and ordered another drink.

"You . . . feeling okay?" Daniel asked, sliding up next to me. "I know this whole party is a little overwhelming, but you're a bit more . . . I don't know how to say this . . ."

"Socially awkward than normal?" I forced a smile.

"Yeah," he chuckled softly, as he touched the side of my face. "We can leave soon if you like. Maybe just another hour? Can you last that long?"

"Maybe with two more of these," I said, clinking my glass against his, "and another smoke."

"That's fair," He chuckled, then kissed my forehead; he was being weirdly affectionate. But to be honest, I really appreciated it. "So . . . you think I should grow a mustache?"

"Daniel," I said with a not-too-subtle warning in my voice.

"I always thought you liked younger guys." He was grinning.

"Knock it off." I felt my cheeks flushing again.

"Oh, come on. You have to let me tease you a bit. Do you have any idea how red your face was?"

"I beg you, Daniel, just drop it."

He leaned in close. "That Thomas guy was really checking you out as well."

"Kind of," I said with a sigh, happy we were switching gears a bit. "Weird, right? Like, they're newlyweds, and his wife's a total babe."

"You're a total babe, too," he chuckled, pulling me in a bit closer.

"Not like her," I shook my head. She was a bona-fide ten, while I'm riding in the six-seven range lane.

"So what did you guys talk about outside?" he asked.

"Nothing, really." I brushed off his question, not wanting to bring up the whole warning thing. Out of context, I didn't think it would make much sense, and there wasn't enough time for a full explanation right now. "Why, you jealous?"

"Very." He kissed me on the lips this time, softly and quickly.

***

After catching up with his parents and being introduced to a bunch of people who honestly all blended together, I excused myself to find a bathroom. Before I left, I whispered to Daniel to meet me outside for a smoke in twenty, then we could leave. He gave my hand a squeeze before I made my way out of the ballroom.

The first bathroom I found was packed full of ladies touching up their hair and makeup, so I doubled back and decided to hunt another down. I figured that a place that big had like . . . hundreds, so finding another one wouldn't be too difficult. I decided to head upstairs since most people seemed to have congregated on the first floor.

After climbing the grand staircase, which I was ashamed to say winded me a bit, I took the hallway to the left. Because, for some reason, the hall to the right was giving me *Overlook Hotel* vibes. The hallway was way too large and lined with floral arrangements similar to the ones outside.

As I walked, I checked every door, all of them unlocked. None of them seemed to be bedrooms. One looked like an art gallery, another a cocktail room, a cigar room, a library, and so on. I made a mental note to return to the library, as it would be way easier to kill a few minutes there then back down at the party. I pressed forward, and *finally* found a bathroom at the end of the hall.

It was smaller than the one downstairs, but not by much. There was a small entrance with a circular chair, about five mirrors and a long very sleek sink beneath them. It smelled of hibiscus and fresh fruit. After I took a piss and washed my hands, I gave myself the once over in the bathroom mirror.

Lena had done my hair and makeup for me. And to give the woman credit, I did look better than I normally did. And it must have been good quality stuff, because I still looked fresh, and my hair had yet to lose the beach waves she had given it. As I admired my appearance, which was something I rarely did, a sudden gust of cold brushed against my neck. I looked around to see if there was an open window or something.

There was none that I could see.

When I looked back to the mirror, a puff of mist escaped my lips. Did someone just turn on the AC on full blast? There was a sudden loud clang, which made me turn around. It was coming from the hallway. As I approached the door, another noise followed it, but this time it sounded like something heavy had fallen to the floor. It was very much like what I had heard the night prior.

Now, you'd think I would have learned my lesson and would know better than to investigate and follow the noise. But the hallway was my only escape route, and the bathroom was growing colder by the second. I weighed my options, but before I could come to a decision, I heard something stir behind me. Then there was a brushing against my ear that felt like long fingernails.

My breath caught in my throat.

Slowly, the talons encircled my ear until one slipped inside. There was a soft hiss that sounded almost like a laugh, then a sudden, sharp *sting*. I cried out, bolted for the door and didn't look back. But I heard it moving behind me, felt the cold air pushing against my back. Its long nails, I knew they weren't far behind, waiting to snatch me away.

I rounded the corner. Knowing I was almost to the staircase, for a moment, relief coursed through me. But that was when I ran right into something hard. Large hands gripped my arms, stopping me from falling to the ground.

I looked up into a pair of stunning blue eyes. The silver fox.

"You truly have no patience, my dear," he spoke, but not to me, he was looking past me, to whatever that thing was behind me. "Not that I blame you." He looked back at me. His cool eyes seemed to penetrate every pore in my body. I wanted to run away and yet, at the same time, I wanted to succumb. "She is a delectable morsel." He drew me in close, his right hand moved up my shoulder, my neck, caressing my face.

I tried to speak, but before I could, his lips engulfed mine. His tongue was hot, so much so, it practically burned. Tears filled my eyes as my vision blurred. His hand moved from my cheek, gripping my hair tightly, while his other hand explored my body. My legs went weak. I could barely breathe. I had never felt anything like this before. Heat built deep within my loins. I wanted him, more than I ever wanted anyone or anything in my life.

When he ended the kiss, I could no longer stand on my own. My every limb, every joint felt heavy. My breath was haggard, my vision fading. I felt his hand moving back to the side of my face, caressing me softly. My lips parted, and out of them came words that I can't explain. But I knew, at the time, that I meant them.

"Devour me," I begged.

He chuckled. "Not yet my pet . . . but soon."

Kissing me, once more. This time softly. Teasing me.

Till everything turned black.

CHAPTER SEVEN

That Was My Second Guess

Waking in an unfamiliar place was always a little disorienting, but waking in an unfamiliar place after being chased by a creepy Ring girl, and then making out with a sexy older guy before passing out was something out of a hallucination. How much did I drink last night? Not to mention the throbbing headache, the full-body chills or the earth-shattering realization that my life was officially crazy.

It took me a full minute to realize I was back in my in-law's house. I looked around in a panic, for or a second thinking I was still in the sexy creepy man's mansion. I called out for Daniel as I stood from the king-sized bed. My legs were like jelly, but I powered through. Wobbling around, I found a robe resting on the edge of the bed. It looked like it was for me, and I was still cold, so I slipped it on.

Then the door opened, Daniel appeared with two

coffees and a scowl on his face.

"Here." He handed me the black beverage, then walked out onto the balcony. I followed suit in silence, trying to gauge his mood. I wondered how much he knew, how he had brought me back to his parents home. I decided to wait for him to talk first.

He handed me a cigarette, then slipped another between his own lips. "So, what happened?" he finally asked, after lighting up both of our smokes. "You were fine. You were drinking, but it didn't seem like you had much. How did you end up passing out?"

"Okay . . ." So he didn't know I made out with the silver fox. It was understandable that he would think it was because of alcohol, but I needed to quell that thought. And I needed to tell him everything, no matter his reaction. "This might sound crazy . . . but I want you to hear me out."

"I know this has all been overwhelming. Trust me . . . I get that," he interrupted, causing my lips to tighten up. "But were you sneaking shots or something behind my back?"

"What? No, I . . ."

"Riley, is this all really so bad?" he interrupted again, the hand holding his cigarette was trembling slightly. "This is a good opportunity for us."

"Wait . . ." A lump formed in my throat. "What do you mean . . . a good opportunity?"

"Look," He said, taking a long drag. "There are lots of powerful people here, many with influence, who I could make connections with. I mean, why, Riley? Why did you have to pass out in front of Mr. Beelze? Of all people? Do you know how that makes me look? How it makes my parents look?"

"Daniel, I wasn't drunk. I . . ." I started.

"You've been acting really weird," He interrupted me yet again. "I've been trying to be understanding, but last night crossed a line."

"Would you just listen for a minute?" Heat rose in my face. "Mr. Beelze, he . . ."

"He what?" Daniel stubbed out his cigarette. "Caught you when you fell, carried you to a private room then came and got me, so I could sneak you out without everyone seeing?"

"He did more than that." I was trying very hard not to raise my voice, I knew if I started yelling, he wouldn't believe anything I said. "Daniel, there's something really strange going on here, with this whole place."

"Riley, stop." He held up his hands. "Honestly, I just want you to admit you drank too much, apologize, so we can move on."

"Please, Daniel, just listen for, like, five seconds," I reached out to touch his arm, but hesitated. "Weird things keep happening to me."

He made a face but didn't say anything.

"The first night I stayed here, I got out of bed and down the hall, there was, like, this thing. Like a person, but not. It looked like the creepy chick from the *Ring*. You know, the one with the long black hair? And, she was, like, coming at me. That's why I booked it, that's why I brought the priest over."

His face was turning red as I spoke. But I couldn't stop.

"Last night, when I went to the bathroom, she . . . it . . . that thing . . . was there again. I ran away and bumped into that Mr. Beelze guy . . . and he like . . . talked to it, like he knew it or something. And then all of a sudden, I got dizzy and everything went black."

A chilling silence surrounded us. He looked me up and down. I could tell there were a lot of thoughts forming behind those baby blues, but I had a feeling that none of them were in my favor.

"So . . ." he started, slowly. "You're saying there's what . . . a ghost haunting you or something? And you think Mr. Beelze has something to do with it?"

"Yeah, believe me, I know it sounds crazy . . ."

"More than crazy, Riley," He turned, walked off the balcony and back into the guest room. "And since when have you believed in ghosts?"

"I don't know . . . I mean if that's what it is then . . . I guess I believe in them now. But you're missing the point."

"And what is the point?" Daniel was reaching the end of his rope – I'd seen it before. There was only so much arguing he could stand before fleeing.

"Mr. Beelze talked to it, and I think he did something to make me pass out. I promise you; I was fine. I mean, besides being chased by that thing. I was tipsy, maybe, but nowhere close to passing out. But then I bumped into Mr. Beelze and just like that, I was getting weak and dizzy."

"Riley . . . look, I didn't say anything when I got here. But my parents told me you drank a lot that first night."

"Not any more than they did!"

His eyes told me he didn't believe me. "Last night too . . . maybe you drank more than you could handle."

"You have no idea how much I would prefer it being that simple." How could I make him believe me? "You think I'm lying to you?"

"I think you weren't clear in the head." He was walking to the door; he was going to leave. "I think you thought you saw things you didn't."

"Daniel . . . when have I ever . . . I mean ever, done anything like this before?" I was desperate, and he wasn't listening. "Think how distressed . . . how scared I'd have to be to run to a church, of all places! You know me, Daniel!"

"I do know you." His jaw was clenched, his hand on the door knob. "You never liked my parents. Maybe them moving here . . . finally having success . . . maybe that bothers you."

"Daniel . . ." I started to talk but stopped when he flashed me that look, the one that told me I'd better drop it, I did. And he left, slamming the door behind him.

I knew him believing my story was a long stretch. If the roles were reversed . . . I probably wouldn't have believed him either.

***

I dressed in the clothes I had come in two nights prior. They were freshly washed and pressed; I might add. I managed to get out of the house unseen. Daniel wasn't the only one who needed a break. I didn't have a game plan.

All I knew is that I wanted out of Lilith's Gardens. I walked down the street slowly. It was mid-morning and there were a few guys in crisp, matching jumpsuits out and about clipping bushes and mowing lawns.

My walk went undisturbed, right up until I was about to reach the front gate. I heard a car slowly pulling up behind me, so I moved off to the side, as one does, not really looking back. Or at least, until I heard someone calling out my name. I turned around and spotted a bright red Lamborghini and a crooked-nosed face that I didn't really care for.

"Out for a walk?" Thomas asked, a beaming smile on his mouth.

"Is that what it looks like?" I said, frowning.

"If you're headed somewhere, can I give you a ride?" If this man smiled any wider, I was certain his cheeks would tear.

"No, thanks." I slowly started walking again. "If I wanted a ride, there are apps for that."

"Yes, but a ride from me would be free." I cringed internally when he winked.

"Would it?" I cocked my brow at him while he just kept on smiling. Under normal circumstances, I would never have gotten into a car with a guy like him, but these weren't normal circumstances. He had warned me about Mr. Beelze . . . so there was a possibility I could get him to tell me more. "Fine, but no being creepy."

"I'll try my best."

As I sat down in the car, his wide grin somehow grew wider, "So, what's our destination?"

That was a good question. I thought about asking him to take me back to my apartment, but I didn't want to be that far away just in case Daniel decided he was up for a talk. That's when the handsome face of a certain priest popped into my head. He had listened to me once . . . maybe he would again?

I gave him the address and we were off.

"So where were you headed?" I decided to start with some small talk before I asked him fifty questions.

"Was going to pick you up, actually," he said with a chuckle, but that wasn't funny to me. "I saw you leave your in-law's house and hopped in my Lambo, and well . . . here we are."

"Remember what I said about being creepy? Like five seconds ago?"

"And I said I would try," he countered. "But to be fair, the creepy behavior started before you asked me. Nothing I can do about what has already transpired."

I had no comeback. When you're right, you're right.

"How does your wife feel about you stalking other women?"

"Who?" His brows rose as if he was genuinely confused.

"The blonde-haired vixen you married like, what, a week ago?"

"Ooooh, her," he said, still smirking, while I was annoyed. "We have an understanding, of sorts."

Swingers . . . I knew it.

"Not completely like swingers," he said, somehow reading my mind. "Our marriage is really more for . . . appearance."

"Like her daddy's rich or something?"

"Or something," he said, not really answering my question, but I wasn't mad.

Wasn't my business anyway.

"Well, for the record, I'm very married and most definitely not a swinger, so . . ."

"Don't worry, Riley. I know that. But that doesn't stop me from liking you any less."

"Well, you're not going to get anything out of it," I warned him, leaning back in the carbon fiber seats that smelled like polish and too much money.

"Wasn't really looking to get anything out of it." He flashed me a quick glance before looking back at the road.

"So, why stalk me? Why offer me a ride?" *Why warn me about Mr. Beelze and that . . . meditation room thing?*

"Riley, are these the questions you really want to be asking me?" he inquired, as if reading my mind yet again. "You don't have to beat around the bush."

"Maybe I like beating bushes?"

He let out a short laugh, which was followed by a questioning look as if he was waiting for me to get down to the serious questions.

"Okay, fine . . . why did you warn me about Mr. Beelze?"

"I think you have some idea why already," he replied, coolly. "You did a good job following my warning, by the way. Top-notch."

So he knew what happened last night?

"Hey, it's not like I was out there actively looking to cross paths with him. I just kind of ran into him."

"Ran into his mouth, more like it." He laughed in a way that almost made that statement sound light-hearted, but a pit formed in my stomach.

"How do you know about that?"

"Just assume for the time being that I know everything about everything and that will make this easier," He winked.

" Trust me."

"I don't know what happened." I felt my face flushing red. "I mean, I didn't . . . I'm not like that."

"No, you're not." His tone seemed kinder all of a sudden and it threw me off. "And that wasn't your fault. Trust me . . . I don't know if I want to tell you why. Just know that it isn't."

"Why don't you know if you want to tell me?" The car started to slow, we had arrived at the church.

He looked out the window at it for a while, then looked back at me. His golden eyes were serious, for a moment. But then that Cheshire smile returned. "I'm still deciding just how much I like you, Riley. How much I'm willing to tell you."

We made eye contact for an uncomfortable amount of time, like we were playing chicken: loser talks first. While staring at him, I came to the realization that I hated how handsome his face was. Even with the snout, it was a little too perfect. It was the kind of face you wanted to slap, maybe punch – anything that would somehow ruin it, even just a tiny bit.

"Any other questions before you head inside?" he asked, breaking the silence.

"You want to come with?" I really hoped he would say yes because I wanted to get help from Lawn and I was pretty sure he didn't believe me much last time. I figured he just came and did that house blessing thing because he felt sorry for me. So, if I had Thomas to back my story up, maybe he would be more down to help me.

"In . . . there?" He looked at me like I was crazy for a second.

"Where else?" I countered.

"Why don't I wait for you here?" he said, after a momentary pause.

"Look, I . . . I really need help right now. And trust me, normally you would be the last person I'd ask for help. But with everything that's going on right now, it's like . . . insane. And you seem to be the only one who knows what's going on and is willing to help me."

"Riley, I'm not sure that it would be a good idea," he replied slowly.

"Thomas," I reached out, touching his hand lightly. "Please..."

Before responding Thomas looked at the church, then back at me. Back at the church. Back at me. "All right . . . Riley, there's something about you that just . . ." he said, his golden eyes searching my face. "I'm starting to worry about how much I'm drawn to . . . how much I like you."

"Yeah . . . umm, okay," I replied, as I removed my hand from his and stepped out of the obnoxious luxury car. "But could you, like, not?"

***

From the moment we crossed the church's threshold, Thomas turned from annoyingly suave and cocky to a sweaty mess. He kept adjusting his collar, clearing his throat. And in all honesty, I thought he looked better that way.

"It's really hot in here, yeah?" He struggled to smile.

"Is it?" I raised my brow. "I think it's a little chilly if anything."

"No? Maybe it's just me then?" He looked at me and winked.

I rolled my eyes and continued looking around.

"So why are we here?" he questioned, as we walked around a seemingly empty church. I had peeked into Lawn's office and hadn't seen him, so now I was just kind of loitering, hoping to run into him.

"Looking for Lawn," I replied, curtly.

"Lawn?" Thomas said, then cleared his throat again.

"He's the priest who works here . . . lives here? I don't know, whatever priests do in churches."

"He's the one you brought to your in-laws?" Thomas's voice cracked as he spoke. He sounded awful, and if I gave half a shit about him, I would have been concerned.

"Yep."

"And what will finding him accomplish?"

I shrugged. "I'm kind of making this up as I go along."

"Riley, I love your laid-back, no-nonsense attitude. I really do."

I had never seen a man sweating quite this much.

"But do you think we can maybe not walk around here aimlessly? I'd like to leave as quickly as possible."

"Why?" I tilted my head slightly. "Worried you're going to burst into flames?"

"More or less," he said, chuckling, but quickly turned it into a cough.

"Don't worry," I said, smirking slightly, despite myself. "My atheist ass hasn't burst into flames, so I think you're fine."

"If only that were true," He seemed to force his smile.

I was about to tell him to wait outside when I heard someone behind me.

"Riley?"

I turned and saw Lawn's perfectly proportioned features twisted in surprise. Clearly, he had thought he'd never see me again. If only he were so lucky. I ran up and had to force myself not to hug him. I wasn't sure why but seeing him was revitalizing.

"Lawn, I am soooo happy to see you!" I turned to Thomas, who was slowly following me. "This sweaty man is Thomas, by the way, but you don't have to worry about him."

"Isn't she sweet," Thomas laughed, even though he was

looking like he was about to puke. "It's nice to meet you, Father . . . Lawn?"

"Lanh, actually," Lawn corrected him, with a small smile.

“W-well,” Thomas cleared his throat, his every word sounding painful. “I-it’s nice to meet you, Father Lanh.”

“You as well,” Lawn gave the sweaty man a glance up and down look before focusing his gaze on me. "So what can I help you with, Riley? To be honest, I'm surprised you're back . . . and so soon."

"Would you believe me if I said you converted me and I'm here to join your congregation?"

He raised his brow in response.

"Okay, I'm kidding," I relented quickly. "But I might need your help with the weird ghost thingy again."

Lanh looked me over, then Thomas, who offered him a sweaty grin.

"Alright, I'll bite," Lawn shook his head. "Why don't we head into my office?"

"YES!" Thomas exclaimed, making both Lawn and I jump. Then he cleared his throat, "Yes, I think we should do that."

Thomas practically sprinted to the office. Lawn and I exchanged a look before following after him. Thomas was waiting for us at the door, and as soon as we entered, he shut it. He was suddenly a lot less sweaty, but he still looked a bit frazzled.

"Would you like some water?" Lawn offered, as he gestured for us to take a seat.

"Do you have whiskey?" Thomas asked, as he sat down. "Not much of a water guy. You know, fish poop in there."

"I'm afraid not," Lawn shot me a look, asking me with his eyes who I had brought with me.

I just shrugged in response.

"So, Riley," Lawn continued, as he took his seat. "I think I might have mentioned it before, but I'm not exactly in the ghost hunting business."

"I think your exact words were that you're not a ghost-buster," I corrected him.

"And they still ring true."

"But you helped me once," I interjected.

"Yes," he replied slowly, "I did."

"So, you might as well help me again."

"Her logic is flawless," Thomas said, beaming.

"So," I looked at him with the most innocent eyes I could muster. "What do you say?"

His look was stern at first, but melted rather quickly, "Okay, Riley, how about you tell me what happened, and then I'll decide."

***

He listened in silence the whole time I talked. It was kind of nice not being interrupted every sentence or two – I wasn't used to that. The less sweaty, but still uncomfortable Thomas paced around as I talked, like an animal locked in a cage. I noticed that he kept glancing at the top drawer of Lawn's desk.

"When I was leaving, I ran into this guy," I gestured toward Thomas, who flashed Lawn a pained smile. "And now we're here."

"I see," Lawn looked back and forth between the two of us, then sat back in his chair, "So what do you think happened exactly? Do you think this . . . Mr. Beelze . . . drugged you, or something?"

"I don't know . . ." I had never thought of that, which surprised me. Why was I so set on this being something supernatural? I looked over at Thomas and he shook his head as if to tell me, *no you weren't drugged.*

"And this *Ring* girl you keep seeing . . . what do you think she is?" he asked, his dark eyes piercing.

"Again . . . I don't really know."

"So . . . what do you want from me . . . exactly?"

Good question.

"I don't know . . . I just . . . I need help, and I don't know where else to go. If this is something . . . I don't know. . . supernatural. Then maybe you could help me?"

"Riley," he replied slowly, "I don't want to say anything that might hurt you but . . . both times you saw this . . . entity. . . you were drinking, yes?"

I didn't like where he was going, but I nodded all the same. After all, it was true. I had been drinking both times, but I know my limits. And Thomas said I wasn't drugged. So whatever it was that I saw, for the time being, I have to believe that it was real.

"Do you think it's at all possible that you might have drank too much, maybe . . . fallen asleep and had a nightmare?" He leaned closer to me, the look in his eyes screamed concern, not judgment. "Again, I'm not saying this because I don't believe you. You think you saw something, and it scared you. But sometimes our minds play tricks on us, and yours wasn't in a clear state, to begin with."

"She's got a clearer head than yours, pal," Thomas said, clicking his tongue. "This is the guy you think that can help you, Riley, seriously?"

I gave Thomas a sour look that shut him up.

"Look, Lawn, you don't really know me. And I get where you're coming from but trust me when I say I'm not someone who's ever believed in life after death, in any sense. To me, ghosts and things that go bump in the night were pure fiction. Something for entertainment purposes and just that." I tried to make my face look as sincere as possible. "If I knew what was going on, I'd tell you, but all I do know is that whatever is going on in Lilith's Gardens isn't normal. And, I have a feeling my husband and I might be in danger. So please . . . at the very least, do you think you could come with me to talk to this Mr. Beelze guy? I need to prove to my husband that things there ain't right. But I can't do this alone. I need you, your holy water, maybe a cross or two. I don't know. Something for protection."

"That's your plan?" Thomas interjected. "I told you to stay away from Mr. Beelze. Not to rush into the lion's den head first!"

"So this Mr. Beelze is dangerous?" Lawn asked Thomas.

"What?" Thomas smirked coldly. "When she tells you, you don't believe her, but now that I say something, you do?"

"Thomas, back down. I know I asked for your support, but I don't need a white knight."

Thomas pouted in a way far too childish for someone with such a mature face.

"It's just annoying. "Trust me, you're barking up the wrong tree. This guy can't help you. His blessing at your in-law's house didn't work. So why do you think he can help you with Mr. Beelze?"

Good point. But I didn't know who else to turn to.

"Okay, I don't know what's going on," Lawn stood up, his full attention now on Thomas. "But you seem to know more than what you're saying. If Riley and her husband really are in danger, we should contact the proper authorities."

"What, like cops?" Thomas released a hearty laugh. "You've heard her story. You really think they'd be able to help with that? Guns aren't gonna work. Arresting people won't work either. Trust me."

"Give me a reason to trust you," Lawn challenged him.

Thomas made a noise of disgust. It was my turn to stand up. I walked over to Thomas and put my hand on his arm. It worked last time, so I figured I might as well try it again.

"Thomas, I know you said you weren't sure how much you wanted to help me. But if you have a way of showing Lawn that I'm not lying . . . that I'm not going completely insane . . . please. Can't you just show him?" Maybe I was just tired, maybe I was desperate. But I felt my eyes filling with tears.

"Riley." His voice was low. "You don't know what you're asking of me. I've already done too much. Risked too much. Any more than this and I . . ."

"Thomas," Tears started rolling down my cheeks. I wished I were faking it, that I wished I were just manipulating him. God, I hated crying, but I was exhausted and confused. "It's not just about him . . . I need to know I'm not going crazy. I need proof that this is all really happening. If not, I don't know how much more I can take."

He reached out, wiping a tear from my face. Normally I would have swatted his hand away. But again, I was fucking desperate and this was all a complete mess. Thomas looked at the tear on his thumb for a moment, then looked deep into my eyes. A sly smile curled across his lips.

"It just keeps amazing me how much I'm willing to do for you," he chuckled, then turned to Lawn. "Lanh, in the right drawer at the top of your desk, there's an old trinket of some kind that holds value to you, yes?"

"I . . . well, yes. There's an old cross from my Grandmother . . ." Lawn's eyes widened in surprise. "But how did you . . ."

"Just get it, priest," Thomas commanded.

"Did you bring a magician with you or something?" Lawn asked me with a small smile, as he extracted a really beat up cross from his desk, then placed it on top.

"Maybe I did . . ." I said, looking at Thomas with a raised brow.

Thomas, looking sweaty and nervous again, walked over to the desk.

"It just had to be a cross," he grumbled more to himself than either me or Lawn. Then he looked at me. "I hope this doesn't make you like me less."

"That would be impossible."

"I'll take that," he said with a wink that made me audibly groan. Then he took a deep breath. He reached his hand out; I noticed he was trembling. The closer his fingers got to the cross, the more he quaked. Lawn flashed me a confused look that I replied to with a shrug. We both turned our attention back to Thomas, who looked more and more disheveled. Finally, after what felt like an eternity, he grabbed hold of the cross.

From his enclosed fist spilled ink-black smoke. His hand trembled violently; it was so so much that it traveled up his arm before coursing through the rest of his body. From deep within his throat came a ferocious growl. It was a sound that you would expect to come from a wild beast, not from a human man. But it wasn't the trembling or the growl that disturbed me the most. No, it was his eyes, which were wide and filled with pain. I watched with a slack jaw as they transformed from that warm honey brown to a thick ink-black that slowly trickled out, filling even the whites of his eyes. He released the cross, letting it tumble across the desk. He held out his hand towards Lawn, who now had his back pressed against the wall. The flesh of his hand was blistered and burned, in the shape of the cross he had been holding.

"Do you believe her now, priest?" he asked, in a voice that no longer sounded like his. *No, perhaps this was his true one.*

It was like something straight out of a horror movie. Really, I should have been pissing myself. I didn't know if it was because of everything that had happened to me the past few days, but what I felt in that moment wasn't akin to terror. No, it was closer to relief. I wasn't crazy. And now, looking at the trembling Lawn, I felt like I wasn't alone.

"I knew it!" My perhaps overly-excited tone broke the defining silence that had filled the room. "You guys are vampires!"

Lawn looked at me with wide eyes, his mouth agape. I heard a deep chuckle, and looked back at Thomas, who was slowly starting to look less like a monster.

"Vampires? Really, Riley?"

"No?" I asked, feeling my face flush a little . . . Stupid, Riley. Come on, girl! I thought we put that theory to bed! "Well . . . I mean the cross and the flesh burning thing, classic vampire situation, you know?"

"It's also classic demon possession." His eyes were back to their golden hue, and now with only his hand trembling, it seemed he had enough energy to wink at me. "Wouldn't you agree?"

"Oh," I said sheepishly. "That was my second guess."

"Sure, it was," he said, laughing, at least until a loud crash brought our attention back to Lawn, who was now on the floor. His body was a crumpled mess, his eyes rolled up to the back of his head. I ran over to him, quickly supporting his head, I looked at Thomas for help.

"See," he said, shaking his head slowly while placing his hands on his hips. "This is exactly why I don't reveal myself to humans."

CHAPTER EIGHT

Shit is Crazy . . . So for Now, Let's Just Drink . . . Deal?

An unconscious priest in the trunk . . . sounded like the punch line to a bad joke. But nope, for me, that was just another Monday, apparently. Because there I was, driving in a Lambo with a demon, a passed-out priest in the boot of the car, fifteen minutes away from my apartment. Honestly, I should have been in full panic mode. But I was surprisingly calm.

Maybe it was the comfortable seats, the smooth drive or the cool night air that seeped through the small crack in the windows. Or the fact that despite being a demon, Thomas was a very studious driver.

"You're sure he's not gonna die back there?" I asked as I looked through the rearview mirror toward the trunk.

"Nah," Thomas said dismissively. "There's plenty of air, and besides, he's still unconscious. Won't be awake for at least another hour."

"You sure?"

"Trust me," he winked, as I crossed my arms. "We demons have a way of knowing these things."

"Riiiiiight," I grumbled, looking out of the window, feeling his eyes on me for a second, then turning back to the road. "So . . . is Thomas your real name?"

"Why do you ask?" I saw him smiling in my peripheral and instantly regretted my question.

"Well, it's not a very . . . demonic name."

"Yes, I suppose it's not," he said, chuckling. "Thomas is the name of the man this body belongs to. We tend to go by the names of the bodies we acquire."

"How come?"

"It's just better that way," he answered simply.

"Is it?" I glanced at him. "I would find it confusing to have to change my name all the time."

"You get used to it," He said, still smirking at me. "Besides, we can't exactly go around telling everyone our true names. That would end badly for us."

"Why?"

"Our names are powerful," he said after a moment. "If people know them, they could . . . make us go away."

"Oh." I touched my finger to my chin, thinking. "And how does that work exactly?"

"Well . . ." He glanced at me, then smirked. "When our true names are spoken, we have to obey the orders of the speaker. No matter what they ask, we must comply."

"So, if I knew your true name, I could command you to leave the body you're in right now? And you would have to do it?"

"That is correct."

"Okay, so you know all the other demons at Lilith's Gardens real names, right? Including Mr. Beelze?"

"Yes, I do," he cooed.

"Would . . . you tell me their names?"

"Nope," he said, casting me a wink. "But nice try."

"How about the names of the two that got my in-laws?" I figured it couldn't hurt to ask.

"Riley, I really can't," he replied in a sorrowful tone, like he actually felt bad or something. "That kind of goes against our code."

"Well, we can't go against demon code, I guess," I said, flashing him a small smile. "How about your name then? Can you tell me that? You know . . . just in case I want to make you go away?"

He laughed. "I would, Riley, but I'm worried you'd make me leave right this very second."

"I would at least wait till we got back to my apartment . . ." I was cracking jokes with a demon – what was happening to my life?

"I'm happy you're not too freaked out by all this." This I could tell, because he was grinning from ear to ear. "I've made friends with other humans through the years, and I have to say, you've taken the demon reveal better than, well . . . all of them."

"Okay, just to put this out there, you and I ... are not friends."

"Yet," he said, offering me yet another wink.

"Gross," I said, rolling my eyes. "Anyway, I don't want you to think I'm all fine and dandy with you and the whole demon possession thing. Honestly, right now, I'm just happy that I'm not crazy. This whole situation is still a complete dumpster fuck. And I'm not thrilled that you're in another person's body right now – it's creepy."

"But Riley." His voice cracked like a teenager going through puberty. "He gave his body to me willingly . . . promise."

"And why would he do that?" I asked, skeptically.

"He wanted money, wealth, a Lambo . . . you know, all that stuff you humans are basically trained to desire. And in exchange for those things, I got his body . . . and his soul."

"So that's how this whole thing works? You demons promise people to get them the things they want, and in exchange, they give you their bodies and their souls? They know this, and they're okay with this?"

"Well, not exactly . . ." He looked at me with puppy dog eyes, which I did not care for. "We might fudge the details a bit, but they definitely know that we're getting their souls for all eternity."

"So basically, these people are trying to sell their souls to get shit that they want," I clarified. "Then you guys just go in and take their bodies as well?"

"That's how the rest of them do it."

I could tell he was carefully watching my reactions.

"I told my guy that he had to give me his body for five years, and when he woke up, he would have everything he desired."

"And then you get his soul for all eternity?"

"Well, Hell does . . . yes." Maybe he could tell I didn't like what I was hearing, because he quickly added, "But this guy was going to Hell anyway."

I cocked my brow.

"I mean, he probably was."

"So what, he just let you come into his body . . . just like that?"

"Well, he did sort of freak out last minute and run away,"

Thomas replied, almost sheepishly.

"So he changed his mind?" I shifted in my seat, crossing my arms over my chest defensively, with the sudden urge to tell him off. Then, not for the first time, I wondered how I had found myself in this situation.

"Yeah, well," He looked a bit uncomfortable too, which was weird, now that I knew what he was. "But he had already entered the meditation room, so . . . At that point, there's really no going back."

I considered asking him for more information about the meditation room, but we were pulling into my building's parking lot, so I decided to hold off on that question and directed him to Daniel's parking spot. Once out, we opened up the trunk. Lawn was curled up and still very much unconscious. Thomas reached in and removed the white-collar from his shirt before picking him up, princess-style.

"His collar?"

"Thought it would look a little weird if anyone saw us carrying a priest up to your apartment," he explained.

"No, I totally get that. I just thought the white thing was part of the shirt already." I shrugged. "You learn something new every day."

"Some of them are built-in."

"But not his?"

"Nope, not his."

***

"You have a cat!" Thomas exclaimed as he dropped Lawn on the ground with a loud bang.

"What's the matter with you?" I ran over to the unconscious priest and checked his head for bumps. Luckily, there were none. I took a second to admire his fantastic bone structure before turning my attention back to Thomas. "I know you're a demon or whatever, but you can't just drop people like that."

"But . . ." he whined as he crept slowly toward my cat, who was inching away from him with her back arched. "She's so fluffy."

"She doesn't seem to like you much. Which is weird, as she's usually friendly."

"It's not weird at all," he said, holding out his hand for her to sniff, causing her to hiss. "Cats are very intuitive; she knows I'm not human. Cats never like my kind, but I've always loved them."

"Okay . . ." I mumbled, while watching him pathetically try to get closer to her. "Do you think you could help me get Lawn to the couch, or are you just gonna keep doing that?"

"It's always been my dream to pet one," he mumbled, as if in a trance.

"Okay . . . you're being weird again," I crossed my arms. "Can you knock it off, you're stressing her out."

"Alright, I'll stop," he said, pouting. "But, umm . . . what's her name?"

"Cat."

"Very straightforward," He flashed me a crooked smile. "I like it."

"Lawn. Couch. Now!"

"Yes, ma'am." He did a mock salute, then picked up Lawn like he weighed nothing.

"And please, place him on the couch. Not drop him."

"I'll try my best," He winked.

I rolled my eyes.

It was starting to become our thing.

***

"No, we will not do that!" I snarled.

"Trust me. No one stays unconscious when you do that to them."

"I don't give a flying fuck! That's just disgusting!"

"But Riley," he whined, pouting his lips and slouching his shoulders. "I'm so bored, and he's been comatose for like . . . forever!"

"No means no!" I snapped. "You ain't doing anything that repulsive in my apartment!"

"I could take him outside?"

"No!"

"S-stop yelling," Lawn grumbled, his eyes still closed, his face scrunched up in discomfort. "M-my head feels like it's about to split open."

"Lawn, how are you feeling?" I knelt down next to him.

"Like I was hit by a car." He opened his eyes, meeting my gaze for a moment before slowly sitting up. When he saw Thomas, his face instantly turned a ghostly white. For a second, I thought he was going to pass out again but after a steady deep breath, he straightened himself up. "So where am I, and why is he here?"

"My apartment, in Manhattan," I explained, as I glanced at Thomas, who was standing a little bit away with his arms crossed, pouting. "And he's here because . . . I don't really know why."

"You know why! I've told you, it's because I like you."

"Right," I grumbled, slowly. "I kind of wish you didn't, though."

It sucked when he was just some tall, dark, and handsome guy crushing on me and wouldn't take no for an answer.

Now that I was aware that it was actually a bloody demon crushing on me, it sucked on a whole other level. Like there had to be something really, really wrong with me for a demon to like me so much . . . right?

"Soooo . . . why am I here . . . in your apartment?"

"Well, you kind of, sort of, passed out. After the whole cross-demon-burning incident."

"I vaguely remember that part, yes."

"And I didn't want to just leave you there, all unconscious and stuff. Plus I still kind of need your help . . . so here we are."

He looked at me for a moment, his dark eyes searching my face. "I need a drink."

"Oh, yeah, sure," I stood up. "What do priests drink? Like water?"

"Something stronger, please." He covered his face with his hand, he really didn't look good.

"Whiskey's fine?" I asked, even though I was already at the bar pouring three drinks.

He nodded in response. I gave Thomas his glass first and he flashed me a wide grin. Ignoring him, I sat next to Lawn and handed him his glass. He took a large gulp that was soon followed by coughs and wheezing.

"I said something strong," he said, slowly."Not lighter fluid."

"Hey, hey," I cooed, touching his shoulder. "I know you're

probably reeling, maybe having an existential crisis, but we don't insult whiskey in my house."

"Sorry," he chuckled humorlessly.

"It's okay," I said, sipping my drink. "I'll let it slide this once . . . because I need your help and stuff."

"Can I talk to you for a second?" he said, casting a quick glance at Thomas, whose full attention was back on Cat. Even though my cat was suffering, I had to admit I was happy he was paying attention to something other than me. "Alone."

I nodded and we walked to the balcony together. Thomas didn't even look at us, as he was crouched down now, eye level with Cat. Her fur was sticking up straight. Once outside, I offered him a smoke. He hesitated for a second, but then accepted. I lit it up for him, and he coughed after taking in a drag.

"It's been a long time," he chuckled, taking in a more successful inhale.

"How long?"

"Probably . . . wow. Twelve years?" He looked up at the city sky, which was splashed with rouge and vibrant coral. I watched the smoke curling up from his full lips. I couldn't decide if he had a nice profile or if it was just his crazy jawline that had me so transfixed.

"Now I feel bad," I remarked, lighting my own smoke.

"Really? About a cigarette?" he smirked. "But you're cool with throwing me at demons?"

"Well," I smirked back. "Isn't that kind of your job?"

"How are you so . . . okay, with all of this?" He took another sip of his drink, that time he didn't complain, although he did wince.

"Oh, trust me, I'm not," I leaned against the rail, taking a long drag. "I'm just relieved I'm not crazy, and that I finally have some support. I don't want you to take this in a bad sort of way, but I was a hard-core atheist. I didn't believe in ghosts, or anything supernatural. You live your life, then you die. That's all there ever was for me. Then I saw that thing and honestly, my mind has been going on hyperdrive ever since. Because either I saw something that wasn't there and I was losing my mind, or everything I thought I knew was a lie. And at the time, I didn't know what was worse."

He nodded, and I found myself admiring how carefully he always seemed to listen.

"But I think a part of me knew it was the latter. That I wasn't crazy, or at the very least I held some hope. I don't know why . . . that despite my lack of faith . . . the first thing I did was run straight to a church . . . straight to you."

"I'm not sure I can help you, Riley." His smile was soft, thoughtful. "I'm not . . . I don't think I'm the right person for this. I'm just a priest with a small congregation. Yes, I've been trying my best to live my life according to God but . . . I'm just one man."

"That's okay." The smile on my face, I really meant it, even if it kind of hurt. "If you can't help . . . I mean . . . It's just nice to have another person . . . well, human person, be here, and believe me."

"Well, I was presented with some compelling evidence," he chuckled as he looked at his own palm. "That was some . . ."

"Freaky shit?" I laughed.

"Couldn't have said it better myself." We touched our glasses together.

"Let's drop the whole 'demon community, my in-laws are possessed, and my husband's with them alone right now' thing." I offered up my best smile. "Shit is really crazy . . . so for now, let's just drink. We can figure out the rest later . . . deal?"

"Deal." His eyes reflected the setting sun in a way that made my stomach do a weird flip- flop thing I didn't much care for. He was too close, not wearing his priest collar thing, and smelled surprisingly good for someone who had just been stuffed in a trunk. But before my train of thought went too far down this totally inappropriate route, it was luckily interrupted.

A blood-curdling scream echoed from within my apartment. Lawn and I exchanged worried looks before running back inside.

CHAPTER NINE

Whether or Not It's a Bad One, It's Still the Plan

As soon as we ran through the balcony doors, we stopped dead in our tracks. My beautiful friend was in the middle of my living room, screaming at the top of her lungs, a can of pink pepper spray in hand. The burning liquid coated Thomas' face. Though Thomas looked mostly unaffected by this, he certainly didn't seem happy.

"Human, please, stop spraying me," Thomas asked nonchalantly.

Andrea refused to listen.

"Andrea!" I called out, still not wanting to get closer because the smell of that shit alone made my eyes water.

"Riley!" She looked over at me with red puffy eyes.

Clearly, pepper spray was meant to be used outside, not in a cramped Manhattan apartment. She stopped her onslaught and ran over to me, wrapping her arms around me tightly. "Oh my God! I thought you weren't here! I came to feed Cat and when I walked in, there was this strange guy and . . . oh my God, I'm so sorry! Is he your friend?"

"It's okay." I patted her back gently. "It's actually pretty badass how ready and willing you are to pepper spray a guy in the face. And he's not my friend . . . and he's a demon, so don't feel bad, okay?"

"Riley." She broke our hug and tried to wipe her tears away with her sleeve, which probably contained pepper spray residue because her eyes only became redder. "It's not nice to call people demons."

"But, he is one." I smirked at Lawn, who still appeared a little dazed.

She turned to Thomas, who was drenched in pepper spray and wearing a half scowl.

"I'm so sorry," she apologized, even though she looked more in pain than he did. "I thought some guy had broken in here. If I had known you were a friend . . . acquaintance . . .of Riley's, I never would have done that . . ."

"Yeah," Thomas' response was surprisingly curt, as I thought he would crack a joke or wink or something. "Don't worry about it. Though, you probably will."

"Why don't you wash up?" I said, dragging her to the bathroom. "I'll bring you a change of clothes."

"Umm, yeah, okay." She kept looking at Thomas, clearly feeling guilty. "Again, I'm sorry."

I closed the bathroom door, then turned to Thomas, "So pepper spray doesn't hurt demons, huh?"

"Nope," he said, suddenly looking like his annoying self again. "Maybe if it were blessed but, I don't know if that would work either, honestly. Don't think anyone ever tried it."

"Maybe we can have Lawn bless it, then do a retest?"

"By retest, you mean spray me with it?"

"See any other demons here I can test it on?"

"How about we do something that smells nicer than this stuff," he suggested. "Maybe we could try your perfume? I wouldn't mind smelling like you."

"Ew," I said, crinkling my nose. "What did I say about being creepy?"

"Believe it or not, I'm really trying."

"Whatever," I sighed. "Go wash up in the sink, I'll grab you one of Daniel's shirts or something."

As I walked toward my bedroom, I turned to find Lawn behind me. He half nodded toward the room. Guessing he was asking if it was okay for him to enter, I nodded. Once inside, I headed straight to the closet, shifting through to find something that might fit Andrea and Thomas.

"Do you think it was a good idea to tell your friend that Thomas is a demon?" Lawn asked.

"Probably not," I shrugged, as I pulled out an oversized sweater and leggings. "But I'm going to explain everything anyway. She's my best friend, I tell her everything."

"But then she'll be involved," he pressed on. "What if we can't trust Thomas? I know he's helped you thus far, but he is still one of them. If he knows that she knows, then her life could be in danger."

"I . . ." Hadn't thought of that, why hadn't I thought of that? Did some weird part of me trust Thomas? *Why?* Because he gave me a warning? *Because he had let himself be burned by Lawn's cross?* Those weren't reasons to trust him. Not so completely. "You're right . . . but still. I've never lied to her. If she asks me, I know I'll tell her."

"Can't you just . . . not?"

"It's not that simple," I said, shaking my head, as I rummaged through my husband's shirts, looking for something simple and cheap. "She's literally the only person I'm one hundred percent honest with. When she's around, I have no filter."

"Yes, but," Lawn paused, "for your friends' sake, can't you just not tell her? Don't lie . . . just don't say there's a demon in your apartment right now and that your in-laws are possessed, and your husband might be next?"

I released a reluctant sigh as I turned around, ready to agree with Lawn. Then I saw Andrea standing in the doorway with her mouth hanging slightly open. Lawn followed my gaze, paused for a moment, then looked back at me.

"Well," He finished his whiskey with a grimace. "Never mind."

***

Andrea had come into the bedroom to ask for a towel. After giving her one, she returned to the bathroom without asking a single question, though it definitely looked like her mind was reeling. And when she finished, she walked straight to the bar and filled a highball glass nearly to the top with whiskey. She then went and sat next to me on the couch. I was on my third cigarette, Lawn his second glass of whiskey, and Thomas was back to staring at Cat. Though now he was wearing an old tee-shirt Daniel had won in a silly carnival game that read *FBI – Female Body Inspector*... I thought it suited him.

After Andrea took a long sip, she turned to Lawn, "We weren't properly introduced. I'm sorry. I was distracted by all the pepper spray."

"That's fine," Lawn replied, looking suddenly bashful.

"I'm Andrea." She held out her perfectly manicured hand.

"Lanh," He couldn't have crossed the room to take her hand faster if he tried.

"It's nice to meet you, Lanh," As if she were seeing him

for the first time, I saw a small smile creeping across her lips. “Though I’m sure I didn't make the best first impression. I’m actually kind of embarrassed.”

“Don’t worry about it.” Lanh’s eyes never left her face. “In your shoes, I probably wouldn't have acted much differently.”

His words were followed by silence and more smiling. I had seen her look at guys like this before, and it was never a good thing. And even though he was a priest, he was basically looking at her the same way. I made a mental note not to let them have too much time together. I needed my priest sin-free and ready to fight demons. Not having a taboo romance with my best friend.

Not that I blamed him. Or her. Andrea was the whole package and then some.

And Lawn was not without his charms.

"So," she finally spoke, but the sexual tension clearly remained. "That guy over there . . . he's a demon?"

Lawn nodded.

"Like not just a guy who's kind of an asshole. We're talking biblical demon. Drag-your-soul-to-Hell demon?"

"Yep," I chirped in, "and he's a bit of an asshole, as well."

After swearing in Spanish, she took another long drink.

"Not really into the dragging souls to Hell business myself," Thomas stood, finally giving Cat some respite from his advances. He walked in front of Andrea. Their gazes met.

For . . . a bit too long. Like he was looking for something in her eyes. Then his nose scrunched up as if he smelled something rotten and he said, "I'm surprised you're so ready to accept all this."

"W-well," Andrea shifted uncomfortably then looked at me with a soft smile. "Riley never lies to me . . . so if she said you're a demon . . . then . . ." She finished her sentence by chugging the rest of her drink.

"Watch yourself, little lady, drink that any faster and you might choke," Thomas said in a way that made me think he kind of did want her to choke.

"Well, now that everyone's on board and all caught up with this unusual situation," I said, in an attempt to get us back on track. "Why don't we come up with a game plan?"

"A plan for what, exactly?" Lawn's brow furled.

"Relax, Lawn, like I said – tonight we'll just relax and drink. But I still need to come up with a plan. I can't just leave my husband in a pit full of demons, now can I?"

"I wouldn't really call Lilith's Gardens a pit," Thomas interjected. "It's more like a luxury resort full of demons . . . if anything."

"So . . ." Lawn complexion turned off green. "You want to go back there?"

"Yep."

"Are you insane?"

"Debatable, but what did you expect when I asked for

your help?"

"To help your husband, yes, but not to go into a whole community full of demons," Lawn shook his head. "As far as we know, he isn't possessed yet . . . correct?"

We all looked at Thomas, who gave us an unsure shrug, then said, "As far as I know."

"Well, if he's not, I think our best option is to get him to leave of his own accord, not rush in there ourselves. Why don't you try calling him to come back here? If you don't think he will believe you about the demons, make up some other excuse."

"I don't know," I said, leaning back into the couch. "He's pretty peeved at me. I'm not sure he'd come, even if I said I was dying."

"Riley." Andrea clasped her hand against mine. "You don't mean that! You know Daniel loves you!"

"Not enough to believe her about all this," Thomas argued.

Andrea shot him a look that I never would want her to send in my direction. Unfazed, Thomas returned the look twofold.

"I wouldn't expect a demon to know anything about love and commitment! Just because they fight sometimes, and just because he had trouble believing her this one time, doesn't mean he doesn't love her!"

"Well, obviously I don't know anything about "*Love*" and "*Commitment*," Thomas refuted, emphasizing his words with finger quotes. "But still, Daniel's super lame for not believing her. And now he's gonna get possessed tonight, and frankly, he deserves it."

"WAIT, WHAT?" I shot up from my seat, as Thomas smashed his lips together, clearly regretting what he had just said. "Tonight? You just said he wasn't possessed!"

"Well . . ." Thomas said, grimacing. "It's probably not happened yet. But if they're following the original plan, it'll take place at midnight tonight."

"When? You? I ... What the hell!" Heat had rushed into my face as my mind went into panic mode.

"I think what she was trying to say is," Andrea interjected politely, "When were you planning on telling us that?"

"Didn't need the explanation, princess, I got what she meant," Thomas said flatly. "And I was never going to tell you ... Well, maybe tomorrow, after the deed was done."

"And whyyyy?" I couldn't stop shouting, I was physically incapable of lowering my volume.

"Because for the first time in my life, I actually agreed with a priest." He gestured to Lawn, who shook his head as if to say, *'Don't look at me.'* I don't want you going back to Lilith's Gardens. If you do, they *will* get you, and *when* they do, there isn't much I can do for you at that point. The demon that wants into your body is a particularly nasty one and there's no way she'll ever let you go. And like I've said before, I like you, Riley ... I'd rather you not get possessed."

"So, you took me away from there, took me to Lawn,

showed him you were a demon, and came back to my apartment just to ... what? Distract me?"

"Well ..." Thomas said, flashing me a cheesy grin, which was soon followed by an innocent shrug.

I released a noise that was somewhere between a shriek and a howl, then polished off my drink. Poured another, paced the room, lit up a smoke and turned back to Thomas.

"Okay, you, no more talking," I snapped.

"But Riley!"

"What the *fuck* did I just say?"

Thomas looked like a puppy being scolded, but I didn't give two shits.

I turned to Lawn, "You are going to go and bless every single one of the water bottles in my fridge!"

"Y-yes, ma'am," Clearly scared of my chaotic energy, he dashed into my kitchen without protest.

"Riley, that is not going to wo ..." Thomas started to say.

"Quiet!" I warned, then turned to Andrea. "You ... you can just sit there and be your perfect self. Have another drink. I'm sure you're super stressed and confused right now. This was a lot to lay on you – like life-changing, earth-shattering shit."

"I'm actually okay, I mean, sure, it's weird to know for a fact that demons exist and possess people. But I've kind of always believed they did, so it's not too, too shocking," Andrea said, standing up and hugging me. "I'm just worried about you."

Oh, my sweet beautiful angel.

"Don't listen to that stupid demon, I'm going to be okay. I'm just going to get Daniel and bring him right back here."

"Riley . . ." Thomas started to protest again, this time I was able to stop him with just a wave of my finger.

"But . . . I want to help." Andrea mumbled against my neck. We broke our embrace enough to meet one another's gaze. Her large dark eyes were starting to water.

"You can help by staying here and staying safe." I gently touched the side of her face.

"Can I stay here and stay safe as well?" I heard Lawn call from the kitchen.

"No," I replied, still admiring my beautiful friend's face.

***

I had ten water bottles all blessed and ready to burn up some demons. A priest who looked like he didn't want to be there. An irritating demon with a fat mouth, but whose help I unfortunately needed. And a beautiful friend holding my fluffy, albeit slightly annoyed cat, waving us farewell at the door.

"Be safe, Riley." Andrea looked like she was struggling

to fight back the tears. "You too, Lanh, I'll be praying for you both."

"Thank you." Lawn cast her a sweet look that she returned.

"And you," All her sweetness dissipated as she addressed Thomas, "Don't you let anything bad happen to them, mister!"

"I'm a demon. Don't assume my gender."

"I, oh, I'm so sorry,"Andrea said, as her face flushed and eyes widened.

"Damn it, don't apologize," Thomas looked exasperated. "Stupid millennials."

I elbowed him hard. "Knock it off and get going."

"But, Riley, she's such a do-gooder! It's giving me a migraine."

"Now!"

"All right." With his head hung, he walked toward the elevator. If he had a tail, it would have been between his legs. Lawn cast Andrea one final look, then followed after him.

"Can I hug you one more time?" Andrea batted her long lashes.

I sighed, holding out my arms. The tears finally spilled out as she practically tackled me. I felt Cat squirming between us. She was not having a good day. If I didn't die or get possessed in the next few hours, I made a mental note to buy her some new toys. The good kind, with catnip.

"You have to come back, okay?" said Andrea, letting me go. "Without you, I'd have no one to brunch with."

"I will try," I replied, still not able to lie. I made my way to the elevator. Once the doors shut, I turned to Lawn and Thomas, neither of them looking very optimistic.

"So, here's the plan! We run in there, holy water in hand, splash every mother fucker we see, grab my husband, maybe my in-laws too, if they're not too ... well ... possessed. Then hightail it out of there and back here to have a celebratory drink," I said all of that in one breath, my nerves starting to kick in. "That's the plan, whether or not it's a bad one, it's still the plan . . . okay?"

They both nodded, as the elevator doors dinged open.

CHAPTER TEN

A Terrible, Horrible Place . . . New Jersey

"Daniel?" I called out into the dark mini-mansion. None of the lights were on when we arrived, but the door was left open. Which yeah, I could understand. Not like demons really had to worry about robbers or anything. "Daniel, where the hell are you?"

"Doesn't seem like anyone's home," Lawn said, stating the incredibly obvious.

"They are probably at the main mansion by now," Thomas hung a little way behind me. "There's less than an hour till midnight."

"Do demons, like, have to possess people at midnight?"

"Nah. It's more for theatrics."

"So why not like . . . three a.m.?" He tilted his head slightly, gazing at me curiously, as I tried to work out what my point was. "You know, the witching hour?"

"Well . . . They're demons, not witches."

"It's also referred to as the Devil's Hour," Lawn remarked, shaking his head. "Isn't it?"

"Trust me," said Thomas, chuckling. "The Devil isn't constricted to one hour a day; he's always working."

Lawn and I looked at each other.

"Anyway," Thomas said quickly, clearly, he had picked up on the tension. "Three a.m. is super late, and although we demons don't need sleep . . . we do like it."

Not that I wasn't completely fascinated by demons and their sleeping patterns, but saving Daniel was a little higher on my priority list, and I was running out of time. Without a word, I ran out of my in-law's house and darted down the street. The Beelze mansion was just down the block and I didn't really see the point of piling into the car again. I heard Lawn and Thomas following me, but I didn't stop until I was at the mansion's entrance.

Unlike my in-law's place, this one was fully illuminated. As we approached the door, I heard the voices of people partying within. And I hated it for happening, but all my gusto vanished as I reached for the door. Even with a bag full of holy water, even with a priest by my side, I had the sudden feeling this wasn't going to work out.

That was when Thomas reached out and touched my

hand. Well, technically, it was the hand of some poor possessed guy I didn't even know. That made my stomach tighten into knots. I kind of felt like I had to poop.

"And, who said it was okay to touch my hand?" I went to give him a stern look, but that quickly dissipated when I saw the concern in his eyes.

How come demons can look like that? Totally not fair.

"I know I can't stop you from going inside, but can we talk for a moment?"

"Kind of in a hurry, you know?"

"I know . . ." He paused, looking at Lawn, who was hovering at the bottom of the stairs. "Can you plug your ears for like . . . one minute?"

"Um, I guess," Lawn complied.

"Think about what you're doing, Riley. Really think about it."

"You don't think I have?" I stood my ground firmly. "I know this is very dangerous. Trust me, I know. But I can't leave Daniel behind. We made promises to each other. I know our marriage hasn't been perfect, no one's is, but I do love him . . . and, he needs me."

"He might . . ." Thomas hesitated, glancing at the floor. "He might have chosen this, Riley. At least to some degree. I know his parents did – they wanted success. They wanted their family name to mean something. Maybe they didn't fully understand the repercussions of their choice. But they did choose it. Daniel might have chosen it, too."

Did he? Did he actually know full well what was happening? Did he pretend not to believe me? Did he bring me here for all of this to happen? He had always been ambitious. He had always wanted more. I knew his parents always pressured him, made him feel like he wasn't successful enough. But that wouldn't make Daniel do something like this . . . *wouldn't it?*

"Riley, is this all really so bad?" Daniel's words rang through my mind. *"This is a good opportunity for us."*

Opportunity, huh? I shook my head. It didn't matter if he knew, even partially what was going on. He was the man I married, and I promised him for better or for worse. And now that I was smack dab in the middle of the worst of it, I couldn't just turn my back on him. No, if I had to, I would drag his pristine white ass the hell out of there.

I stared at Thomas, about to tell him I was going in there whether he liked it or not, but stopped when I saw his soft . . . sorrowful smile. It was like he already knew what I was thinking. He already knew his warning didn't sway me. Fuck, I hated how much he could figure me out. Even if it were just something demons could do. It didn't make it any less annoying.

Thomas leaned in, till his lips practically touched my ear. Then he spoke . . . a word I couldn't understand . . . and yet, I did. Despite being a writer, I had never been good with other languages. That included names. I had always mispronounced people's names, to the point that I just started giving people nicknames. It was easier for me, and less embarrassing. And the word Thomas just said, the sound of it, the cadence, it was like nothing I had ever heard before.

Yet if I opened my mouth, I felt I could repeat it.

"My name," he whispered, a warm yet oddly sad smile crossing his lips. "If things go bad, I want you to use it. But you can't let anyone else hear it . . . you understand?"

"I . . . I mean, I do." I glanced over at Lawn, who gave me a look that screamed, *'What the heck is going on?'* "What will telling me your name do? You're not the one I'm looking to exorcise."

"If you say my name first, then give me a command . . . *any* command. I will have no choice but to listen. Remember?"

"Yeah . . . but like . . . what kind of command?"

"That's up to you," he paused, peering up at the mansion. "I can't go against them of my own volition . . . but I don't want anything to happen to you either. I need you to understand that using my name is a last resort. You can't just go and command me to do any little thing,"

I rolled my eyes. "And what would stop me from making you just tell me all the other demon's true names right now? That would save me a lot of trouble . . ."

"Nothing. But you won't."

He was right . . . again. And yeah, it still pissed me off.

"Whatever, man," I groaned, as I indicated to Lawn that he could unplug his ears. "Hey Lawn . . . before we head in there . . . I was gonna suggest that you wait out here. You know, be a lookout or whatever."

"I would but I'm carrying half of the holy water." He sighed, then walked up the steps to stand next to me. "Besides, I've already been helping you. Might as well keep at it, right?"

"Glad you said that." I patted his back. "Because I was just trying to be nice before. I didn't mean a word of it."

***

I think everyone's had times when they felt like they entered a room and everyone was looking at them. I knew I had, many times. On days when I felt like I looked a mess, or at parties I hadn't wanted to attend. But when I entered Mr. Beelze's mansion, I actually *did* have all eyes on me. The whole room went silent as a bunch of beautiful faces turned my way. I took a step back and felt Thomas's hand on my shoulder.

I looked up at him, but he didn't meet my gaze. He was looking around the room, his eyes black. His face was darker than I had ever seen it. He guided me forward, deeper inside, toward the stairs. I felt the weight of their eyes upon me, with my whole body shaking. I glanced back toward Lawn, whose complexion had turned waxen, following closely behind Thomas. My hand slid into my bag, gripping tightly to one of the bottles of holy water.

At the top of the stairs, we took the hallway to the right. This corridor had fewer doors than I remembered being down the left. On the walls were a shit ton of oil portraits, all of different men, yet they shared a similar quality. Thomas's hand never left my shoulder, which I planned to give him a hard time about later . . . you know, if I wasn't possessed and/ or dead.

At the end of the hall was an obnoxiously large gold door embedded with stones that shone like freaking rubies. As we got closer to it, I made out the door's elaborate design. Like an image from *Dante's Inferno*, it depicted raging fires, horned demons and the faces of humans in pure agony. Thomas stopped me a few paces away from the door, then shouted in that deep, animalistic voice I had heard back at Lawn's church.

"Open the doors, Dolion!"

"Are you sure that's what you want, Ahch?" It was the silver fox's voice, but deeper and far slimier.

I watched as the doors glided open slowly. Seemingly by no one. It was some straight-up Hollywood shit that had me thinking about every time I had screamed, *"Get out of there, you dumb ass white girl!"* while watching a horror flick. Yet there I was, in my *dumb ass white girl* glory, just standing there like an idiot with my knees knocking together.

"Cut the dramatics," Thomas growled. "Just hand over the blonde Ken doll and we'll be out of your hair."

"Why don't you come in and get him?" The silver fox emerged from the pitch-black room, looking all fine. "And bring the girl with you, while you're at it."

"Oh, sure, sounds swell." The levels of sarcasm Thomas reached in that one sentence were fantastic, even by my lofty standards.

"Come now, Thomas," he said, grinning, his eyes now deep dark pools which were focused on me. "Come in and let's have a little meditation session. Once we're all nice and relaxed, things will be so much better. You'll see."

I felt my body begin to move toward the room, but Thomas secured his grip on me and pulled me closer to him. *Why had I tried to enter the room?* It was almost like something had compelled me to move, something outside of myself.

"You don't need this one," Thomas barked. "I'll get you another one."

"But I want that one." He chuckled in a way that made me shiver in fear and excitement.

"Of course you do," Thomas grumbled.

"And what is that supposed to mean?" Silver Fox snapped, turning his attention fully to Thomas. I felt the weird haze that had consumed me somewhat dissipating.

"You always do this," Thomas shot back. "You and *her*! Always, always!"

"And what do *we* do, exactly?" His nose crinkled as he spoke.

"You always possess the humans I like."

"We do not!" He was genuinely appalled.

"You do, too!" Thomas fired back. "What about James?"

"He had a really full head of hair," Dolion huffed. "You know I like my men that way."

"Adaliya?"

"She was really fit."

"Then what about Paul?" Thomas questioned. "He was fat and bald!"

"He had a proud nose," Dolion shrugged, then weirdly enough glanced at me as if I would help him with his argument . . . which obviously I wouldn't.

"Don't you even start!" Thomas howled. "Noses are my thing, they've always been my thing."

"You can't just claim noses in general as your thing," Dolion countered. "That's too broad of a category!"

"Urgh," Thomas said, ruffling his hair. "This is pointless, just give me Riley's husband and let us out of here, all right? You can keep the parents . . . what's done is done. But the boy's young and dumb and you know this isn't very cool, right?"

"He's over the age of twenty-five," Dolion said, turning his nose up at Thomas. "His brain's fully developed."

"Yeah, but we both know men don't really reach maturity till they're like forty . . . if they ever really do." He elbowed me softly. "Am I right?"

I just gave him a wide-eyed look that screamed, *"What the fuck is even happening?"*

"Okay, we're freaking her out and I don't want to do that . . . so can I have him?"

"Thomas . . ." Dolion rubbed his temples. "He's already in the meditation room, he's already submitted, and to be frank . . . as much as you like the girl . . . she was part of the deal."

"She . . . she was?" Thomas looked at me suddenly way less relaxed, I felt my blood turning cold.

"If you came to all the meetings like you were supposed to," Dolion took a step toward us. "You would already know that. *She* and I aren't trying to take a human you like; we wanted her before she even arrived. So if anything, you're trying to take her from us."

"Oh," Thomas started to back away. "Well, that changes things."

"Yes," he hissed, stepping forward. "It does."

It was then I realized we were completely surrounded by possessed people; every pair of eyes black as night. I looked at Lawn, who was trembling like a vibrator on its highest setting. My eyes turned back at the sexy silver fox man, who was approaching fast. That was when I saw a man slowly emerging from within the meditation room.. Daniel! Newly motivated, with a trembling hand, I twisted open the water bottle in my bag, and with a pathetic yelp, squirted as much water on Dolion as possible.

There was a moment of cold silence. As I looked at the now wet, but still sexy super evil possessed guy, a sly smile crossed his features. Then the room erupted with laughter. I watched Daniel, who was standing there silently, not laughing, so I was hoping that meant he wasn't a demon, but his eyes were cold and distant. As all hope of success slipped away from me, I glanced at Thomas, hoping for answers, but his dark eyes were firmly locked on Dolion.

"You really let them bring water blessed by a *murderer* here?" Dolion's laughter joined the rest as my eyes shot to Lawn.

"A what?"

"Riley . . . I," Lawn said but fell silent when Dolion held up his hand.

"And you told them it would work? Ahch, what games are you playing?"

"I was hoping we wouldn't need it," Thomas half-whispered. "I was hoping you would listen to me . . . just this once. I don't want to hurt you. I don't want to hurt *her*. Just let me take Riley, if anything, just give her to me. I'll find you another."

"That won't work." He reached out a hand to touch my face, but Thomas intercepted by grabbing his wrist, and the two demons stared at each other with malice-filled eyes. Then Dolion purred, "We want her. Besides, you promised her to us . . . didn't you, Daniel?"

I stared at my husband with wide eyes, the man I had promised to spend the rest of my life with. And he . . . he just looked away. Tears stung my eyes, but I refused to let them fall. There was no way in Hell I would give a bunch of demons such satisfaction.

Even though the room was spinning, even though so much was happening, I knew I had to act fast. . I couldn't focus on the thought of how much I had totally failed at this rescue Daniel from the demons' plan. How *apparently* Daniel and his parents really wanted this. How Daniel included me in whatever bloody demon deals he had made.

I had even fucked up on getting a priest, as the one *I* found was a fucking murderer! Nope, now was not the time to dwell on that.

I needed to figure out how to get out of there.

But how . . . oh!

"Thomas!" I reached up, grabbing his face, pulling him close to me. In his ear, I whispered the name he had told me as quietly as I could, then I looked into his eyes and said, "Take me and Lawn home."

Thomas' face softened as the largest, most heartfelt smile I had ever seen crossed his lips. He shoved Dolion away, who looked more stunned by this than actually hurt. Then he pulled me in close to him with one arm, then grabbed Lawn with the other. Then he whispered to me, "I need you to think of your home, picture it as much as you can. Pick a vivid memory, one with smells and sounds. Think of a time where you felt safe and hold on to it as tightly as you can." I started thinking of home. The scent of burnt lasagna came to mind, along with the sound of a silly sitcom on television, cars buzzing outside the window, the hot summer sun that snuck through the window curtains and heated the already muggy room. "Close your eyes, both of you! And do not let go of me!"

"Thomas, don't you dare!" I heard Dolion screaming, but his voice soon faded into nothing as everything around me began burning. A wind whipped around me that felt hotter than fire. I held my eyes closed as tightly as I could. My ears rang with the sound of voices, so many of them, all crying out in terror. My throat filled with the cold, hot flames that surrounded me. *Was I also screaming? Was I one of the voices?*

And then it ended, just as quickly as it had started.

"You can open your eyes now," Thomas said, releasing me from his embrace. I took a moment to gather myself, *what the Hell was that?* Then opened my eyes and peered around at my surroundings. We were standing in a dark small room that stank of dust and mold. I walked over to the wall, feeling the cheap wallpaper until I found the light switch and flipped it, illuminating the small living room in which we were standing.

A thick brown carpet from the 'seventies was draped across the floor, where there was a clunky orange sectional wrapped in plastic. The walls covered in tacky patterned wallpaper that burned your retinas. I walked over to the mantle where there was a picture of a small child and her mother.

"Where . . ." Lawn was the first to speak, his voice weak and careful. "Where are we?"

"A terrible, horrible place." I turned to them, the picture still in hand. "New Jersey."

CHAPTER ELEVEN

Fuck No

"Why are we in New Jersey?" Lawn asked.

"I thought of home . . . and for some reason my childhood home came to mind." I stared at Thomas. "We didn't like . . . travel back in time did we?"

"What? No." Thomas laughed like it was the funniest thing he had ever heard. "I can't time travel, Riley, that's ridiculous!"

Note to self, demons don't time travel.

"Why did you ask him if we time traveled?" Lawn chimed in, ignoring Thomas' incessant cackling.

"Well, this place is like . . . exactly how I remember it," I said, taking in the room more closely. "And my mom hasn't lived here for like . . . jeez, over ten years. I knew my uncle had taken over the lease . . . he owns apartments and houses all over Jersey. I just assumed he would renovate this place and rent it as well . . . but I guess he didn't."

I placed the picture back onto the mantel. Uncle Vinnie had seemed so cool and calm. He had handled the funeral, he had helped me move and he had never seemed stressed or upset. I'd always thought of him as calculated and cold. I had no idea he was so sentimental. We hardly ever spoke. Yeah, he sent me a card every holiday, but we hadn't really seen each other since my wedding. And I didn't remember him being around much when I was a kid . . . maybe this was his weird way of showing his love for his dead sister and her child?

"So, if this is your mother's old house," Thomas said, interrupting my train of thought. "That means your childhood bedroom is here?"

"Yeah, upstairs," I said without thinking, then instantly regretted it when I saw his face light up. Before I could even protest, he was bounding upstairs the way a kid bounds toward their gifts on Christmas. I decided to just let him have his fun and turned toward Lawn. He flashed me a worried smile.

"Do you want to talk?" he asked. "I'm sure you have questions."

"Only . . ." I felt I needed to tread lightly here. "Only if you're up for it."

"You're not . . . upset? About the whole me being a murderer thing?"

"What would my being upset help? Besides, I'd rather hear from you what happened before I make any judgments."

"You seemed upset before," he replied softly.

"Well, we were in a bit of a high-tension scenario," I said defensively. "What with the holy water not working, demons surrounding us, and all."

"Fair enough. But you're not the least bit worried about being alone with me after what you heard?"

"Well, we're not alone," I said, a smirk appearing on my lips. "There's a demon here who, unfortunately, kind of seems to like me. So I don't think you'd be able to hurt me even if you wanted to. And more than that, even though I haven't known you long . . . I would be totally floored right now if you told me you were secretly a *Dexter* style serial killer or something."

"Why, don't I seem like the type?" The right corner of his lips lifted slightly, and for the first time, I noticed he had a dimple in his cheek.

"Well, so far, I've seen you so scared you passed out, basically hid behind me and Thomas in the presence of danger and trembled like a small child in front of that Dolion demon guy so . . . no, I don't really see you as a cold-blooded killer."

"Ouch." He faked a wince. "I think you might be the only person who could make someone feel bad that they're not a cold-blooded killer."

We both chuckled lightly, then I walked over to the couch. I sat and indicated for him to join me. From my bag,

I grabbed my pack of smokes. Luckily, there were two left. I offered him one and he took it without hesitation. I lit his and then my own.

"Remember when I told you about my grandmother?" he began.

"You killed your grandma!" I interrupted, my cigarette almost falling out of my mouth.

"What?" He looked slightly taken aback. "Riley, no. Why would you assume that?"

"Right, sorry!" I held my hands up. "It's been a crazy day. I'll shut up and listen."

"Anyway," he continued after a long drag. "She wasn't really my grandmother. She just always felt like one to me. You see, she was a sister at the orphanage where I grew up. She was the one who taught me about God, about right from wrong. She was a good woman, I owe her so much... basically, I owe her everything." He took another long drag, his face turned toward the shag carpet.

"Back where I was from, it was a small community. Poor, and for a young boy, especially one with no family, to survive . . . it was common to join street gangs. Fighting was normal for me back then, and even though my grandmother would scold me and tried her best to help . . . there was only so much she could do. Every boy my age belonged to one of two gangs; the whole town was split. We had areas we could go, areas we had to defend, and some that if we entered, we would get beaten black and blue."

"How old were you?" I asked.

"When I joined?" He took a moment to think. "Eleven . . . almost twelve, I think."

"Fuck," I mumbled as I drew smoke into my lungs. Picturing a beat-up little Lawn brought a tightness to my chest.

"One day there was this kid from the other gang who entered our territory by himself. I was fourteen when this happened, that kid . . . he must have been two or three years younger." Lawn's face darkened and I had the sudden urge to reach out and wrap my arms around him, which was weird, because generally, I hated touching people. "We took him into an alley... we beat him... bad. The leader of our group . . . he broke the boy's leg. He hadn't meant to. But we all heard it. I'll never forget the sound."

His hands started trembling, and my urge to comfort him overtook me. I reached out, before grabbing his free hand, and giving it a squeeze.

Lawn looked at me and smiled sadly before continuing, "The boss panicked, he took out a pocket knife and forced me to take it. I don't know why he picked me. Maybe I was just the person closest to him, but he told me to stab the boy. He said that if we let him go with a broken leg, we would all get arrested. That we had no choice. I begged him, pleaded with him. But he told me if I didn't do it . . . that he would stab me . . . then him."

He released a heavy breath. "I was scared . . . I was a coward."

"Lawn . . ." I wanted to say something, but my mind was empty.

"After . . . after," he gulped, struggling to find his words. "I ran to my grandmother. I can't imagine what she thought seeing me there, covered in that poor boy's blood. But she cleaned me up, and she sent me away to the seminary half-way across the country. That's where I joined the priesthood, and eventually was sent on a missionary trip to America."

We were silent for a beat. My hand was still on his. At that moment, I wished I were one of those people that could comfort others, who always knew how to say the perfect thing for any situation. I bet if Andrea were here, she could make him feel better.

"I tried to live my life in a way that would make up for what I had done..." he said slowly. "I thought I was . . . but, I guess . . . a murderer . . . that's all I'll ever be."

"But Lawn, you were so young . . ." I snubbed out my cigarette on the coffee table, then touched his face, turning it to meet my eyes, "Yeah, what you did was wrong. But it wasn't an action done out of malice. You were scared for your own life, and people do irrational things in those situations. You're not a bad man, Lawn."

"And yet," he whispered, moving his head away, "Clearly my sin outweighs anything good I may have done. My holy water couldn't protect us."

"Holy water is a tricky thing." Thomas was walking down the stairs, and I cursed under my breath when I saw a few photo albums tucked under his arm. "So is sin. Riley's right, you're not a bad person. But that doesn't mean you're qualified to turn water into something that can pierce a demon's flesh."

"So . . ." I saw Thomas' eyes drift down toward my hand, which I realized was still holding Lawn's. I let go quickly, then continued, "Who would be *'qualified'* to make such water?"

"Someone who's been baptized under any religion and who is practically sin-free." Thomas walked straight over to where we were seated and made a gesture for us to move over so he could sit between us. Much to my chagrin, Lawn complied and Thomas plopped down next to me. "The freer of sin they are, the better. The demons at Lilith's Gardens are old and strong. We would need some near saint-level holy water to even hope to combat them."

"Are they of similar strength to your own?" Lawn inquired. I could tell he was thinking up something in that well-structured head of his.

"Well, Dolion's the strongest . . . well, besides *her*. Then me . . . then everyone else."

"Wait, wait, wait!" I held up my hands to stop him from talking. "You're, like . . . the third strongest demon there? Then how come you were all like, *'I don't know if I can help you, Riley.'* You made it sound like they could all beat your ass."

"It's complicated," Thomas said and shrugged, with a shy smile on his lips.

"My grandmother's cross worked on you," Lawn stated.

"So can we assume it would work on the other demons there?"

"Yeah, your grandma must have been, like, crazy saintly," Thomas said, and made a face. "But one cross isn't going to do much. There's too many of them, and all they have to do is not touch it, so... not the most effective weapon."

"She's . . . not still alive, is she?" I asked as respectfully as I could.

"No." Lawn shook his head. "She passed away a few years back."

"I'm sorry." I glanced past Thomas at Lawn, who smiled warmly at me..

"Anyway," Thomas continued, leaning forward a bit and blocking Lawn from my view. "Like I said, it's super- duper hard to find someone who can make even halfway good holy water. But hey, we got out of there. We're safe. How about we just move on and let what happened happen and I don't know, just head back to your apartment in New York, so I can play with Cat more?"

"Wait!" Lawn's eyes were suddenly filled with light. "You said this person could be any religion?"

"Yes," Thomas replied slowly, as if cautious.

"So, they don't have to be a priest, a nun, or anything like that. They just have to not have sinned much, correct?" Lawn asked.

"Maybe." Thomas looked at him with narrow eyes.

"When we were leaving Riley's apartment you told her

that Andrea was *'such a do-gooder'* and *'that it was giving me a migraine,'* right?"

"I'm not sure those were my exact words," Thomas said quietly, almost hesitantly.

This time I stood up, pointing a finger at Thomas. I exclaimed, "And as soon as she arrived you were all cranky! Almost like how you were acting when we were in Lawn's office! I thought it was because she pepper-sprayed you, but it was more than that, wasn't it?"

"It was like her very presence made him uncomfortable!" Lawn said, grinning at me. "Just like the presence of my grandmother's cross!"

"I wouldn't say just as much," Thomas mumbled.

"Oh my God, I knew it!" I raised my arms up in excitement. "I always said my Andrea was an angel!!"

"If she blessed the water," Lawn turned his full attention back to Thomas, "Would it work?"

Thomas shrugged the way a little kid did when they didn't want to admit something.

"Riley, ask Thomas if it would work," Lawn turned to me.

"Would it work, Thomas?"

"Would what work?" He flashed me a goofy smile that had me rolling my eyes.

"Holy water blessed by Andrea?"

"I mean . . ." he said, frowning slightly, "It might work . . . but like I said, this stuff's complicated."

Lawn and I looked at each other, triumphant and hopeful once more.

"Let's head back to my apartment!" I exclaimed, turning back to Thomas. "Can you like, teleport us there? I'll be really careful to think of it this time."

"I'm fine with going back to your place," Thomas stood up and sighed. "But I think we should go the old-fashioned way."

"Why?" I countered. "Your weird hell fire teleportation thing would be so much faster. And an car from here's gonna cost me a fortune."

"I'll pay, and I know it's more time consuming, but I'm not sure it's a good idea to bring humans to Hell and back twice in one day, let alone within one hour."

"H . . . Hell?" Lawn's eyes were so wide they practically filled his entire face. "When w-we teleported b-before . . . that was . . . *actually* Hell?"

"Well, yeah," Thomas said, chuckling. "I'm not like a teleporting superhero or something. Demons travel to places through Hell – it's like our own smoking and burning, souls of the damned being tortured for all eternity, highway."

"Not much different than the New Jersey Turnpike, am I right?" I said, while elbowing Lawn playfully in the ribs. When he didn't respond, I glanced up to see that his face was white as a sheet. "Uh, oh."

There wasn't even time to even yell, 'Timber!' before he was out cold on the ground. At least the carpet was thick and soft. Thomas came to stand next to me as we gazed down at our unconscious priest. Then Thomas gave me a slight nudge and pointed to the photo albums under his arm.

"Can I keep these?" he asked me with wide and pleading eyes.

"Fuck, no."

CHAPTER TWELVE

Won't You Miss It?

It's official, I thought, I am weak. Not like I ever thought I was Wonder Woman or anything, but I used to think I had a backbone.. But after arguing with that idiotic demon for what felt like an eternity but was actually about ten minutes, I relented and let him keep one of my photo albums. At first, I was going to let him pick. But after he made a comment about how adorable I was with my round glasses and even rounder belly when I was like six, I confiscated all the albums of me under the age of ten.

He ended up picking the one album of me in my last year of middle school. When I had braces and . . . bangs . . . *God, what was I thinking?* It was the last photo album my mom had put together of me. I guess I wasn't cute enough to take pictures of after that, or maybe that was around the time she started working all those long hours. Who knew? I didn't like to think about it. But at least the album kept him quiet on the Uber back to my apartment.

Despite the late hour, Andrea was awake when we arrived. Seeing that Daniel wasn't with us, tears filled her large dark eyes as she practically tackled me to the ground with a soaking wet bear hug. I told her everything that happened as we sipped whiskey, then Lawn chimed in, telling her how it seems she would be able to produce holy water that could work on the demons.

"I'm not sure, Lanh, I'm not a priest. I'm not even Catholic," Andrea said, shaking her head. "If your holy water didn't work, why would mine?"

I looked at Lawn, who looked like he wasn't really comfortable with recounting his past to her as well, which I understood completely. They had only just met one another, and a tale of how you were practically forced to kill someone wasn't exactly small talk.

But before I could chime in and come up with some reason why her holy water would work while Lawn's wouldn't, Thomas finally looked up from the album and spoke, "Because despite his career choice, he's a normal person," Thomas explained. "While you're basically a saint."

"W-what?" she stammered. "No, I'm not! I mean I go to church every Sunday but . . . I've . . . you know . . . sinned and stuff."

"Hardly," Thomas groaned.

"I . . . I mean . . . I try to be a good person but I'm far from perfect." She looked at me like she wanted me to back her up, but I couldn't. To me, she *was* basically perfect. "I drink all the time."

"Not a sin . . . as long as it doesn't cause harm to anyone else," Thomas said, before yawning. "And you've never been drunk while driving, never been drunk or even hungover at work, you've never even gotten into a drunken fight with anyone."

“Yeah but . . . Wait, how do you . . .” Andrea tilted her head slightly.

“Ugh, even your choice of career. Everything you do is all about helping people.” Thomas’s lips curled up in disgust.

"But I'm kind of vain, you know," She looked down to the ground. "I post all those pictures of myself online all the time, I've even made money off it . . ."

"And with the money you get from that . . . what do you do with the money you make, missy?" Thomas cocked a brow at her.

"Well, I donate it," she admitted after a bit of a pause. "But that's just because I have a decent job, so it's not like I need the money,"

"Exactly," he said, rolling his eyes. "So you use your appearance, yes, but you do it to help others . . . not a sin then."

"I didn't know you did that." I looked at her with wide eyes, she's an even better person than I thought . . . *Why was she my friend?*

"It's not a big deal," she shrugged, clearly embarrassed.

"And it certainly doesn't make me a saint. I have my flaws."

"Flaws do not a sinner make," Thomas countered.

"But I've had . . ." she paused, looking at Lawn, then looking down at the floor again. "Relations outside of marriage."

"That's not a big deal," he waved his hand dismissively. "Mostly a man-made construct. When it comes to sin, I don't like to get down to specifics with humans because I don't want you to live out the rest of your lives desperately trying to avoid sin. But because you live like that pretty much anyway, I'll let you know that you're way in the clear. I mean you've had sex with what . . ." He looked into her eyes for a moment, then grimaced. "Ew, seriously, only three men and you were in love with all of them? Riley, how the hell are you friends with this person? She's so boring."

"She's not boring! And you better watch what you say about her, or I'll kick you out of here!"

"Riley, don't say that!" He was pouting, but I wasn't having it.

"Then be nice!" I said, crossing my arms.

"But Riley, I'm a demon! It's really hard to be nice!"

"I don't care," I replied flatly, causing him to hang his head in defeat.

"Not that I want to diverge from this extremely important conversation," Lawn chimed in. "But just then, did you read her mind or something?"

"Or something," Thomas said, pouting. "When we first

encounter a human, we can get an overall sense of who they are. We know how much they have sinned, we know what their deepest desires are, but to delve in further we have to look into a human's eyes. Then we are able to see their every terrible thought, their every worry, every single dreadful thing they have done. Or in this little missy's case, every bad thing she 'thinks' she's done."

My mind returned to the party where we had first met, to how much Thomas had been staring at me. *So he had been reading me? Trying to see what a shitty person I was? He knew every awful thing I'd ever done?* Besides being a total invasion of my privacy, it was so unfair. I hardly knew a single thing about Thomas, yet he knew basically everything there was to know about me.

"So," Lawn replied slowly. His cute thinking-face snapped me out of my negative- thought-spiral. "You only can see the bad things people have done . . . their sins?"

"Well, yeah." He leaned back. "I'm a demon, so, we don't really see the good in people, you know?"

"But you could see that Andrea donates the money she makes off of her photos and such," Lawn pointed out. "But only because she feels bad over it?"

"Yeah, she has major guilt over the whole thing for literally no good reason," he said, shrugging.

"Such things are vain," Andrea replied sheepishly. "Even the charities I pick . . . they are causes I care about, which is selfish. There are so many people in need of help and there's so little I can do."

"Andrea," I mumbled. I had never really realized how much she put herself down – I was starting to feel like a shit friend. "Your job is to literally help sick people and you donate all your extra cash to charity! What more could you do?"

"I don't know," she said, softly. "I could be working with the Red Cross, go to poor countries, and help people who truly need it. But I'm here, living in a comfortable brownstone, surrounded by friends and family. I can buy what I want, eat what I want, while there are so many people suffering. It's just not fair."

Thomas let out a noise of both annoyance and disgust. I shot him an angry look.

"You've done more for those in need than I ever have." Lawn looked at Andrea with warm eyes. "And though it might be your humility that keeps your soul so pristine, I wish you knew, at least on some level, just how much better you've made the world, simply by just being you."

"T-thanks," She mumbled, her cheeks had turned deep crimson. "I still find it hard to believe that I can make holy water, or make anything that would have the capability of hurting a demon. But if I can help you guys in any way . . . I will."

"Thank you, Andrea." She and Lawn locked eyes.

"Oooookay," I said a little too loudly. "So this time, we'll have working water – that will help. But we need to come up with a new game plan because our last one was terrible."

"It was your plan," Lawn pointed out slyly.

"Doesn't make it any less terrible."

"Going back there now is an even worse idea," Thomas said, shaking his head. "Besides, Daniel has been possessed already. And let's not forget that this was what he wanted."

"Yeah, it might be what he wanted. He's an idiot, but he's my idiot, so I still have to try."

"Furthermore, and I mean this in the least offensive way possible," Lawn said, meeting Thomas's sour gaze, "we can't just let all these demons continue to possess people like they are. Creating a whole community like this, when will it stop? And even if Daniel chose this, they were going to take Riley by force. Which is why I have a hard time believing that every human in Lilith's Gardens handed their bodies over willingly."

"It's definitely a bit of a grey area," said Thomas.

"I know you're not keen on telling us how all this demon stuff works, but do you think you could at least explain how the meditation room works? Like, you told me that once you enter it, your body is basically served up to a demon on a platter . . . so how does that work?

"Well . . . it's complicated," We all leaned in, our eyes pleading with him to divulge. After a moment he sighed before continuing, "Fine . . . so back in the day, people used to ask demons for shit all the time. And it was super easy to get a body. Like I told you before, Riley, I don't usually keep one human for very long. And back then, it was easy to body-hop. People would come to you for, like, the littlest thing. "*Please help, my crops aren't growing." "My father's making me marry my uncle and he's gross." "My neighbors have better cows than me, please make mine better."*

He paused for a moment, walked over to the bar and poured himself another drink. We watched anxiously, waiting to hear the rest.

"You know, back when just living was really difficult, people were more desperate, and it helped that most of them believed in deities and demons of some kind. But as the years went on and humans became more efficient and focused less on religion, it became harder for us to influence them. I mean, we tried to keep religion prevalent, and it comes in waves, but nowadays, even when people believe, it's more about the principles of the teachings. There aren't enough people who actually think Hell is real or that God is a man sitting on a chair in the clouds. And if you don't think something's real, then you're not going to ask the devil to... I don't know... help you win the lottery or whatever."

"I know a lot of people that are devout," Andrea said, frowning. "Maybe they just don't turn to you demons for help, but to the Lord."

"I'm not here to have a religious debate," Thomas groaned. "I'm just telling you things are different, there aren't a lot of people who believe in their heart of hearts that there are red men with horns and pitchforks living underground. And as a result, there aren't a lot of people lining up to sell their souls to the devil anymore."

"So demons were at an advantage when people interpret religious texts more literally," Lawn clarified.

"It's all about the belief," Thomas said, nodding. "So if people don't think actual physical demons are out there, waiting to ensnare their soul, why would they turn to us in a time of desperation? Who will invoke Satan's name if they think he's just a symbol for the evil of man and not an actual creature that could potentially grant them their deepest, darkest desires?"

"Makes sense," I said, sipping my whiskey.

"Well, I've always believed the devil was real," Andrea countered, "I'm sure there are plenty that still do."

"There are," Thomas said, nodding. "But not as many, is my point. And out of those few, how many are capable of corruption? How many are willing to sell their souls? It's hard to say. So, us demons came up with more . . . innovative ways to be able to possess people. And one of those ways was with what Dolion calls the meditation room."

Oh, the anticipation.

"Dolion first came up with the idea when he was living in India. He had taken over the body of someone who had been on the verge of starvation. Fearful, the man called out to Yama, the god of death. But, of course, it was Dolion who answered his call and possessed him. While in India, Dolion was intrigued by the depth of people's beliefs. Soon he encountered a guru, a man who would meditate for weeks on end. Dolion noticed that in the deepest state of his meditations, it was as if the man's soul would leave his body, as if it would enter a space between life and death. And that gave Dolion an idea.

"He befriended this guru and would often join him in meditation. He studied him over time, and one day, when the guru had fallen deeper into his meditative state, Dolion released his vessel and was then able to occupy the guru's body."

"Okay." I tapped my chin, thinking. "But there's no way I would ever be able to reach such a meditative state, regardless of what room I'm in. Like, if I close my eyes for more than a minute, I'd just fall asleep, or be insanely bored."

"Most would," Thomas nodded. "Which is why Dolion decided to devise a way for humans to reach that state. At first, he tried to spread things like yoga and meditation. You know . . . make them trendy,"

"Oh, Dios Mío." Andrea clasped her hand over her mouth. "My abuela was right! Yoga is devil worship."

"No," Thomas said flatly, shaking his head. "No, it's not. . . But anyway, his plan didn't work, even with people meditating on a more global scale. No one could reach the same state as that guru. So he devised a plan that would . . . help people reach that state. I'm not sure how he did it, as the power within that room is like nothing I've ever seen. But somehow, he was able to create within that room a place where people could physically enter another plane of existence. One where a human can exist both in the physical world, and this place that rests in-between."

"And once in that state, demons are able to enter the body." Lawn ran his hand over his face, clearly contemplating Thomas's words.

"Exactly," Thomas said, nodding. "Once they enter that place, the human body and soul become open, which makes them vulnerable to beings like us."

"Okay . . ." I crossed my legs and swirled my drink around. "I remember you saying that the guy whose body you're in now, that he ran out of the room. But you still possessed him, so how does that work?"

"Once the mind and body are open," Thomas said grimly. "They can never close again, at least not completely. That's why I told you not to step foot in the meditation room. Once you do, you're opening yourself up to all matters of things that you can't even comprehend."

"Yikes," I said, grimacing.

"What would happen if this room was destroyed?" Lawn asked. "Would that free those that have been possessed?"

"Don't know," Thomas said, shrugging. "I would say it's highly unlikely. But this is all new, so I can't say for sure."

"So . . . there's a chance!" I chirped in, exchanging a hopeful look with Andrea.

"A minuscule one, maybe." Thomas' eyes fell down toward the floor.

"Well, minuscule works for me," I chugged down the rest of my drink and stood up. "I'm going for a smoke."

"What do you mean, *'works for you'?"* Thomas inquired. "Even if there's a slim chance that destroying the room would free them, how could we even destroy it?"

"That's a tomorrow problem," Lawn said, yawning. "Riley, you don't mind if I crash on the couch, do you?"

"Go for it, man." I flashed him a thumbs up as I walked to the balcony.

"Seriously, whatever Dolion did in that room, it's something extremely powerful," Thomas continued, "I don't even really know what it is, let alone how to destroy it,"

"Lanh's right," Andrea said, standing up. "We can figure all that out tomorrow. I'm going to crash on your bed, Riley . . . or stare at your ceiling and think about the meaning of life . . . " She stumbled off to my bedroom. Lawn started snoring. I went outside, leaving Thomas alone.

***

"Didn't take you long," I flicked some of the ash off my cigarette.

"Did you want to be alone?" Thomas lingered at the glass door.

"Not particularly," I said, shrugging as I offered him a smoke.

"I brought you another drink." He handed me a glass and took the cigarette. We waited there in silence for a while, and I listened as the cool night air whistled between the tall buildings, hearing the buzz of the cars below. I stared out into the dark night, which was illuminated with the glittering city lights. It was a view Daniel and I had enjoyed many times. Or maybe I had been the only one who enjoyed it, that I was the only one who thought our life together was good. Not great. . . but I had always thought it was . . . at the very least normal.

"Did you know that Daniel wanted this?" I asked, breaking the silence.

"Riley," he said, sighing. "I'm not sure I should tell you what I know. It's all really one-sided. All I get to know about people is the bad. For a long time, that's all I thought there was. But you humans . . . you're complex. For every terrible thing I might have seen in Daniel, there could be a great thing as well."

"I know that," I said, taking in a long drag, "I just . . . I just want to know why . . ."

Thomas gazed at me. I hesitated for a moment, then turned as well, meeting his gaze. It was like I could feel his eyes searching my mind, digging up every worry I had ever had about Daniel. About our marriage, our fights and disagreements. I felt them all bubbling to the surface. And yet I couldn't look away.

"It wasn't your fault, Riley," he said, finally turning his eyes away from mine. "I can tell you that much. It wasn't you."

"Are you just saying that to make me feel better?" I said, resting my elbows on the rail.

"No," he said, smiling softly. "I wouldn't do that."

I chuckled as I took a sip of whiskey.

"If you don't believe me, you could invoke my name and make me tell you."

"Nah." I waved my hand. "That's kind of cheap."

It was his turn to chuckle. "Had a feeling you would say that."

"Well, yeah," I said, snorting. "You basically know everything about me, right?"

"That's not true," he said, smirking as ever. "As I said, humans are complex."

"And you demons are not?" I raised my brow.

"We can be . . ." he mumbled thoughtfully. "But I would say our thought processes are closer to other animals on earth. We are more . . . instinctual."

"Is it, like, an instinctual thing that makes demons want to possess people?" I'd been wanting to ask him for a while why demons were so interested in taking over human bodies, but I didn't want to ask in front of Andrea or Lawn. For one, they were religious and maybe they already knew why. And two, I wasn't sure if this was too personal of a question or not.

"Yes and no." Thomas crossed his arms. "It's more a long-standing desire that we all seem to have and can't quite shake."

"What is that desire, exactly?"

"Well," he said, smiling sadly at me. "I guess we just want to live here . . . on earth."

"That simple?"

"It's not really simple," he mused, shaking his head. "But you had the pleasure of entering Hell for a few seconds today . . . what did you think of it?"

"It was . . ." I shuddered remembering the feeling of the heat on my skin, the cries of pain. "Well . . ."

"Terrible? Awful? Worse than anything you'd ever experienced?".

"Basically," I nodded.

"So, as you can imagine," he grinned, "Not exactly the best place to live."

"I could see that," I frowned. "Still don't think it's cool to take other people's bodies though."

"I agree," Thomas said, closing his eyes. "It's not fair."

"Damn it. Life sucks, dying sucks, and now I know the afterlife sucks as well! I liked it better when I thought that after you die . . . it was just like going to sleep. I love sleep. I can handle that. Being tormented for all eternity in that hot smelly place . . . damn it ... that sucks."

"Well, if you don't go back to Lilith's Gardens," Thomas said, reaching out and touching my shoulder gently. "You wouldn't have to worry about that."

"Yeah, till I die," I inhaled half my cigarette in one drag. My heartbeat increased twofold. I felt the heat on my skin. Spending all of eternity burning in those flames, hearing others' screams, all alone, in pain, alone and afraid.. . . the thought was terrifying. "And with the way I smoke, drink, and eat . . . shouldn't be too far off."

"Riley, you . . ." He stopped mid-sentence, searched my face for a moment, then smiled. "I'll come hang out with you. Make sure no one gives you a hard time."

"In Hell?" I asked.

"After you die, yes." He was still grinning, "That way you won't be alone . . . that way, maybe it won't seem so scary."

"So, bothering me when I'm alive isn't enough for you, huh?" I joked as I tried to ignore this strange warm feeling in my chest.

"Nope, definitely not," he said, laughing. "I'll bother you for all eternity."

"Won't you miss Earth?" I challenged. "Taking over people's bodies, drinking all the whiskey you want . . . won't you miss it?

"Maybe a bit," he admitted. "But I've had all the best whiskeys this world has to offer. Traveled every land, seen every single breathtaking view. I've lived more than enough lives. Knew many fascinating people. And yet, I've only ever encountered one Riley. So, if I had to pick . . . I'd pick you."

I stared at him. The question, *why*, formed on my tongue. But I let it linger there. Because I was afraid of the why. Why was this demon helping me? Why did he like me so much? He returned my gaze and I wondered if he knew what I wanted to say. But then he winked. And I rolled my eyes. Because that was kind of our thing.

CHAPTER THIRTEEN

Spray These Mother Fuckers

I couldn't express how wonderful it was waking up in my own bed that morning. . . well, afternoon, technically. I turned over to find Andrea, her eyes wide and bloodshot, peering up at the ceiling. I reached out and took her hand in mine.

She jumped a bit, then met my gaze with a soft smile. "Finally awake?" she joked.

"Cut me some slack," I groaned. "It's been a crazy couple of days . . . and I did travel through literal Hell yesterday."

"That's fair." She let out a forced giggle, then gave my

hand a squeeze.

"Did you . . . get any sleep?" She sure didn't look like she did.

"I might have drifted off every now and again," she said, her brows furrowing. "This has been . . . a lot to take in."

"Tell me about it . . . " It was my turn to stare at the ceiling with widening eyes. "What is life right now?"

"You have a demon in your living room." This time her giggle sounded real.

"I have a fucking demon in my living room," I said, laughing. As our joking faded, she squeezed my hand again.

"How are you doing, really?" She shifted her whole body toward me. "Are you okay?"

"Okay?" I turned toward her. "I'm trying to be."

She moved in closer, snuggling her head against my shoulder. I hated hugs. . . I really did, but not hers. She was always so warm, so comforting. Sometimes I used to think this was what a mother's hug must have felt like. . . not that I would really know. An image of my mother sitting at the dining room table, looking over a stack of bills came to mind. Her back hunched over; her head supported by calloused hands. No, her hugs probably wouldn't have felt like this. But I bet they would have been nice . . . in their own sort of way.

"Why would Daniel do this?" she mumbled into my shoulder.

I let that question linger in the air for a moment as I

gathered my thoughts.

"He always wanted more," I started slowly. "To be better . . . To make something of himself. His parents . . . they always put a lot of pressure on him. And it seemed like no matter what job he got, no matter how many times he got promoted . . . it was never good enough. Maybe he felt this was the only way he could make them proud . . . I mean they went to Lilith's Gardens first; they met Dolion even earlier than that. I wouldn't be surprised if they influenced him into all this. Not that I blamed them completely. Clearly, Daniel chose this."

"I still have a hard time believing Daniel . . . or his parents . . . would agree to this," she said, trembling a little. "I always thought they were such good people. I knew they were tough on Daniel . . . and you, but I thought it was out of love."

"I think it was . . . in a way."

"If you love someone, you don't try to get them to sell their soul to the devil," she grumbled.

"Well, you wouldn't. I wouldn't . . . but I guess they would."

"You're not serious?" She shook her head as she ended our cuddle session and sat up. "You know I'm a hopeless romantic . . . I've watched so many trashy shows and movies about people falling in love and acting crazy, and I gotta say what Daniel did puts him closer to the husband in Rosemary's Baby than to any love interest in a romcom."

"Relax," I said, laughing. "I was joking . . . mostly."

"I'm going to take a shower," she said, sighing. "Can you make coffee? I feel like my head's about to split in two."

"I'll be right on that, darling!" I saluted her as she grabbed a towel and headed to the bathroom.

***

I walked into the living room with a lit cigarette already in my mouth. I wasn't normally a chain smoker, but the minute I wasn't smoking or drinking, I found myself starting to panic.

Thomas was nowhere to be seen, but I searched the room, until I found Lawn struggling with the coffee maker. I watched him for a few seconds, at his brows, which were drawn in together, his focused dark eyes and his jaws clenched in a way that emphasized the squareness of his jaw. There was a little stubble on his chin and though short, his hair looked slightly disheveled. He hadn't put on his priest collar thing, and I had to admit he looked a lot less stuffy, although maybe that was my own personal bias.

"Need help?" I asked, walking over to him.

"Morning." He looked up and flashed me a toothy grin. "It's a bit embarrassing . . . but yes. I usually drink drip coffee. I've never used one of these. I made two batches already and one was filled with grinds and the other was basically still water."

"Well, good thing I showed up before you wasted any more of my coffee," I teased. I got the pot going in about two seconds flat and noticed him flushing a little red.

"Now I'm even more embarrassed," he said, chuckling. "Looks really easy when you do it."

"Well, it's not rocket science," I peeked at him. "Bet you could even train a monkey to do it."

"Thanks for making me feel better about it," he countered with a shy smile.

"Anytime, man."

We were standing next to each other for a moment, watching the coffee brew, as it filled the apartment with its tantalizing aroma. I heard Andrea turning on the shower.

"Would you happen to know where Thomas is?" I asked.

"He went to get breakfast," Lawn answered. "He left about forty-five minutes ago."

"There's like ten breakfast spots on this block alone. What's taking him so long?"

"You think he's . . ." Lawn paused, "Not getting us food?"

"Oh . . . no, I wasn't implying anything," I reiterated. "I don't think he's gonna like . . . betray us or anything. Knowing him, he has some weird favorite breakfast spot that's like three hours away and decided to get food from there."

"Hope you're right," Lawn shifted slightly.

"Look, I know he's a demon and all," I said, grabbing

mugs. "But if he weren't on our side, I don't think he would have gotten us out of there last time. Like, what would be the point?"

"We don't know how demons think." Lawn watched me pouring coffee into two mugs. "Maybe this is all some weird game to him. I want to trust him, but I think we shouldn't drop our guard. He is still one of them, and he is in someone else's body."

"Only for five years, right?" I handed Lawn a large mug that read, *There's Whiskey in Here.*

"That's what he told us," Lawn sipped the warm beverage. "Doesn't make it true."

"Maybe you're right, maybe we can't trust him. But right now, he's all we've got. And if you seriously want to try and free all those possessed people . . . he's our best shot at it."

"I agree," Lawn nodded somberly. "I just don't want you to trust him too much."

"That's easy," I grinned. "I don't trust anyone . . . well, except Andrea."

"If you say so." He let out a smile. "Just be cautious, that's all I'm saying."

"What?" I challenged. "You think I'm not cautious?"

"Oh, no, you're extremely cautious." The right corner of his mouth turned upward. "Definitely not the type to run headfirst into danger at all."

"Hey! You were right there running into danger with

me."

"Well . . . someone had to make sure you got out of there in one piece."

"Oh, my trembling fainting hero," We looked at one another, then laughed. It felt good to laugh a little.

"What's so funny?" Andrea walked in, somehow looking gorgeous despite the lack of sleep. I was starting to suspect she had a hidden makeup bag in my apartment somewhere, or maybe a whole makeup team.

"Nothing." I poured her coffee into a mug that reads *Hello Beautiful* and passed it over.

"Thanks." She surveyed the room. "Where's Thomas?"

"Getting breakfast," Lawn answered.

"Oh." Andrea's brow furled as a small frown painted her lips, but right then the door busted open and there Thomas was, with a huge bag filled with bagels and another containing various cream cheeses and jams.

"Good morning, humans!" he said, grinning. "I bring you sustenance."

"Where'd you go?" I asked, taking one of the bags from him. "Lawn said you were gone for, like, almost an hour."

"Well, there's this really great bagel spot about half an hour from here," he started to explain.

"There's a great bagel spot like two seconds outside of this very building," I said, as I flashed Lawn an, *I told you so,* look.

"Yes, but this place makes their own apricot jam, Riley! Apricot jam!"

***

"So what are we doing here?" Lawn asked.

"Getting our battle gear."

"At . . ." Lawn looked around, his brows drawn together. "At a dollar store?"

"Where else do you think we can get water guns in the middle of winter? I mean, we could order them online but I don't really want to wait a few days . . . honestly, the longer I'm away from Lilith's Gardens, the less I want to go back."

"Not going back." Thomas appeared behind me holding a bunch of cat toys and snacks. "I like the sound of that."

"Hey." I gave him a quick up and down look. "We're here for demon hunting supplies, not that junk."

"It's only a dollar," he said, smiling sheepishly.

"Each," I cocked my brow. "Shit adds up fast."

"I'll pay?" he offered.

I looked at my cart full of water guns and balloons, then back at all his junk and nodded, "Fine, put it in the cart."

The cheesy grin on his face made me regret giving in.

He dumped everything in the cart and dashed off again, probably to get more useless crap. I looked over at Andrea, who's eyes looked a little out of focus.

I was about to say something when Lawn interrupted my train of thought. "I'm going to step out and make a call. I've been absent for a bit too long and I'm sure Father Tran is freaking out. Honestly, I should have called him sooner . . . or answered one of his many, many calls or texts . . . but I'm still not sure what to say."

"Tell him you're on an incredibly important mission for the Lord?" I offered with a shrug. "I mean, that wouldn't be a complete lie. I'm sure, your God or whatever, would be happy we're trying to get rid of demons, right?"

"Yeah, guess I shouldn't tell him I was stuffed in a trunk while unconscious and taken to Manhattan, huh?" he said, chuckling. Out of the corner of my eye, I saw Andrea snap to attention, her eyes now focused on me.

"Yeah . . . I'd appreciate you leaving that part out," I said, scratching the back of my head. In all honesty, with everything that had happened since then, I had totally forgotten we had done that.

After Lawn left, Andrea turned to me with a cocked brow, "You stuffed Lanh in a trunk?"

"In my defense, he was unconscious and we only had Thomas' Lambo." I flashed her a crooked smile that caused her to cross her arms. "You know . . . they only have two seats."

"Riley . . ." she said, sighing. "That's really dangerous.

And if he was unconscious for that long . . . you probably should have brought him to a hospital."

"He's fine," I said, waving my hand dismissively but she cast me another look and I relented, "But next time we will go to the hospital . . . promise."

"You think it will happen again?"

"Oh . . . I know it will," I said, laughing.

"So," she flushed a little. "I know you haven't known him long, but . . . what's his deal?"

"Deal?" I give her an up and down look. "His deal is . . . he's a priest."

"Well, yeah . . ." She looked away sheepishly. "How devout is he?"

"Andrea," I shook my head. "Look, normally I wouldn't really care about you trying to seduce a priest . . ."

"I'm not going to seduce him!" She blushed a little. "He's just . . . kind of cute."

"Let me finish." I crossed my arms. "But I request that you wait until all this demon business is done. I don't know if it would be a sin to steer someone away from their faith, but it could be. And I need to keep you all clean and pristine till we resolve this . . . my husband being possessed stuff, okay?"

"Okay . . ." She batted her eyes at me sweetly. "I was just saying he's cute. I don't mean anything by it."

"Cute or not..." I frowned, shaking my head. "Hands off ... till we got Daniel back. Deal?"

"Okay. It's not like I planned to really pursue him . . . but I don't see anything wrong with some harmless flirting."

"Andrea, someone as hot as you can't flirt harmlessly."

"That's not fair," she said, pouting in a way I knew and loved so much.

"You looking like *that* is what's not fair," I teased, as I rubbed a hand on her arm. "Making the rest of us look bad."

"Shut up." She elbowed me. "You're beautiful and you know it."

"I . . . I'm not . . . whatever." My face turned a few shades rosier, despite the sudden blast of the air conditioner. *What store does that in the middle of winter?* "Let's, umm . . . let's go to the cash register before Thomas comes back with more useless crap."

"Riley," she said, grinning. "Take the compliment."

"I don't want to."

"Riley."."

"Acknowledge how pretty you are."

"Riley."

"Oh God," I started to walk away, ignoring Andrea, as well as this soft buzzing behind my ears that almost sounded like my name. "Stop."

"Come on, Riley," she said, giggling.

"Riley."

"Do you hear that?" My throat had grown tight, making it almost painful to talk.

"Hear what?"

"Riley.","

"Riley?" Andrea called out to me in concern, as I felt my body start to shake, it was so fucking cold.

"Riley."

Who the hell was calling me? I looked around frantically, as my veins seemed to turn to ice. That soft buzz turned into a steady ringing, chanting my name over and over till finally, it reached a nearly deafening precipice, *"Riley, let me in!"*

My vision started to blur. I felt like I was sinking, deep into ice-cold water. I saw Andrea calling out to me but her words fell mute on my ears. I wanted to reach out, for her to pull me out of this cold, unforgiving darkness. That same voice that had been chanting my name . . . now it was laughing. Filling this icy void, taunting me as I sank down further . . .

But before everything around me completely faded, a strong, warm hand grabbed me, pulling me into them, bringing me out of that relentless darkness. Back into the dollar store that smelled like plastic. I glanced up to see Thomas, his eyes black, teeth bared in an animalistic fashion. Never had I been so happy to see that obnoxious crooked nose.

I followed his gaze to see Dolion standing at the end of the aisle, an unconscious Lawn tucked under his arm. *Of course he was unconscious again . . .*

Andrea let out a yelp as the voluptuous blonde grabbed her from behind, wrapping a slender arm tight around her neck. From within my soul erupted a wave of anger that quieted the cold that threatened to envelop me. *How dare this bitch manhandle my Andrea?*

"Oh my," the sex kitten purred. "I like this one. So clean. So pure. I'm going to have so much fun dirtying her."

"Get off her!" I tried to move in their direction but Thomas held me firmly in place with a strength I found frustrating.

"Riley, try not to move," Thomas warned me under his breath.

I would have snapped back . . . but my body felt unbelievably weak . . . still so very cold. But even more than that, there was something in his tone that made me painfully aware that he was . . . scared.

"Thomas." Dolion walked slowly toward us. "Don't you think it's time we end this little game? She's willing to forgive you for this . . . minor indiscretion. But it's time for you to come home with us, to rejoin our family."

"Home? Family?" Thomas said, and snorted. "I swear you sound more human with each passing century."

"At least I don't insist on making friends with these small, stupid vermin!" he spat.

"Vermin whose bodies you take," I snarled. Thomas's grip on me tightened as Dolion's attention went to me. His eyes turned completely black as they bore into me.

"Yes. Bodies we take and put to *much* better use."

"Enough of this! Tell her to stop," Thomas pleaded. "She knows it won't work. Tell her to leave!"

What won't work?

"You haven't given us much of a choice," Dolion said, smirking. "We tried to take her body the nice way, and we still can if you comply with us. Otherwise, we will take her the old-fashioned way."

"Riley, let me in," it was that voice again. I covered my ears but that didn't help as the voice was coming from within. *"Why fight, Riley? Just let me in, and it will all be over."*

"Thomas, it's in my head," I said, my voice trembling.

"Just hold on to me." His arms felt so warm, almost hot as if they were clashing with the cold that was growing within me. "Dolion, please."

"Please?" Dolion snarled. "Now who sounds like a human?"

"If you struggle, we will take your sweet Andrea," the voice threatened me. *"The priest too. Oh, all the fun we will have with them."*

"Don't you touch them!" I cried out, my eyes clamped shut, my arms and legs shaking so violently that I would have collapsed to the ground without Thomas's support.

"Don't talk to her, Riley! Try not to listen." Thomas was clearly panicking. "Dolion, you know her body won't survive this!"

"Then none of us will get her, I suppose," he said, smiling crookedly. "Which is a real pity . . . Though, I suppose, ultimately, fairer."

"Riley, why not give in? What do you even have to live for?"

Don't listen, I told myself. *Breathe through it.*

"Dolion, why go this far?" Thomas tried to reason. "You have nothing to gain through doing this."

"We could accomplish so much together . . ."

"You've been running around doing what you wish for far too long, Ahch." Dolion was standing inches away from us and dropped Lawn to the ground, then grabbed Thomas by the throat. "Frankly, we are tired of your insolence . . . besides, as I told you before . . . We want her."

"So why don't you give up and let us have you?"

"We," Thomas challenged. "Don't you mean *she's* tired of my insolence. Don't you mean *she* wants her? What do *you* want, Dolion?"

"What do I want?" He let out something close to a villainous cackle. "What she wants!"

Gripping Thomas's neck even tighter, he pulled him in then launched both of us down the aisle. Thomas took the brunt of the fall, keeping his body firmly around me till we landed. He placed me on the ground before turning back to Dolion. He charged back down the aisle, his fists clenched, but Dolion was ready for the onslaught and knocked Thomas against the shelf, causing both to go flying toward the storefront.

I struggled to my feet, trying my best to ignore the relentless nagging that filled my mind. I hobbled toward Andrea and the boobalicious demon-babe, who was at least somewhat distracted by Thomas and Dolion knocking over shelf after shelf, completely trashing my favorite dollar store. If I weren't in so much pain and desperately trying to save my friend, I would have been concerned for the store owner, who, fortunately for them, seemed to be MIA.

"You can't save them ... you're far too weak. But let me in, and I promise no harm will come to them."

Yeah, right.

I reached out and grabbed a chunk of the softest, bounciest hair in the world and gave it a sharp pull. She turned to look at me, a clown-like grin plastered across her perfect features. I instantly regretted all of my life choices as she grabbed hold of my shirt and pulled me in close. What exactly had my plan been? Pull her hair . . . and then what? I wasn't a lover per se, but I was definitely not a fighter.

"Riley!" Andrea whimpered.

"You're a strong one," sexy Goldilocks mused. "I get why she wants you so much."

She lifted me by my shirt off the fucking ground, with those twig-like arms! If I weren't so terrified, I'd be super impressed. Andrea struggled to get free as I dangled there like a newborn kitten in their mother's mouth. I was mentally preparing myself to get launched down the aisle again when a large baseball bat came down onto Valley girl's head. She dropped me to the ground and turned toward her assailant.

Lawn stood his ground; bat ready to swing once again.

"They're going to die, Riley, and it will be all your fault."

Ignoring the demon in my head, who was really starting to grind my gears, I charged forward, tackling Pamela Anderson with all the force I could muster. Much to my surprise, as well and Andrea's, Lawn's, and the demon's, I was able to get her to the ground. Her grip on Andrea finally relinquished. Andrea scurried up and grabbed my arm and yanked me from the floor. Lawn hit her with the bat on the head again. And again, and a third time.

"Water!" I grabbed Andrea's shoulders. "We got to get bottled water, like now!"

"Riley, even if we do, I don't know if I can actually . . ."

"You've got this!" I cut her off. "You kind of have to!"

She nodded and dashed down the aisle toward the fridges in the back. I glanced over at Thomas, who was being knocked around like a rag doll. I cursed under my breath as the bodacious demon babe stood up. Lawn looked at me for any idea of what to do, but really I was just going to try tackling her again. I mean, it had worked the first time. Luckily, Andrea rounded the corner with two water bottles in each hand. She stood next to Lawn and began praying over the bottles. Her words seemed to disturb blondie, who began to stagger and cover her ears with her hands.

Even the voice in my head seemed affected as it

screamed, *"Shut her up, it won't work! It's a waste of time – she will die. So will he, and it'll be your fault! It'll be because you didn't let me in!"*

"Oh my God, shut up!" I yelled, then I turned to Andrea. "Spray these mother fuckers!"

Andrea nodded, tossing a bottle to Lawn, then pointing hers at Jessica Simpson, she bumped a decent portion on the liquid onto her face. The demon recoiled, and her pale flawless skin began to blister. She let out a terrified cry as she scrambled to get the water off herself. Lawn fumbled, grabbing one of the water guns. He filled it as quickly as he could, then dashed to Thomas' aid. He sprayed Dolion . . . and Thomas a bit, unfortunately. Though, in his defense, they were more or less a tangled mess of fists and blood at this point. They broke apart and released several cries of pain. Dolion growled – reeling back, I saw that he was about to launch himself at Lawn. But before he could, Lawn squirted the bastard right in the face.

Thomas, ignoring his own burning flesh, ran through the completely demolished store . . . RIP Dollar Store . . . grabbed the water bottle from Andrea, and ran to me. With his free hand he gripped my shoulder tightly. He was looking straight into my eyes, yet I knew it wasn't really me he was looking at.

"Get out of her," he growled. "I don't want to force you out."

"There's only so much I can forgive," I heard her speaking within me. *"You've pushed us too far this time."*

"I know," Thomas' brows furled. "I didn't even think I would go this far."

"Then stop this." The voice was softer now, almost a whisper. I didn't feel cold anymore. A strange numbness was spreading through me. *"Let's end this nonsense. Let's go home, Thomas."*

"I . . . I can't," Thomas smiled sadly. He tilted my head up, bringing the water bottle to my lips.

"I won't let you have her." This time it was me he was looking at. I wanted to say something . . . but I didn't know what. My feelings were all jumbled, I didn't even know if they were mine . . . or hers.

"Drink," he commanded, and I nodded and gulped down the rest of the bottle's contents. It felt like I swallowed down straight up hot sauce. And I'm not talking about regular hot sauce like Red Hots or Sriracha. I'm talking the strong stuff, made out of ghost peppers or Carolina reapers. I heard the demon in my head let out a painful scream and all the cold left me and was replaced by a burning fire.

Kind of felt like I was in Hell again, but this time it was on the inside.

"What did you do?" Dolion let out a piercing cry.

"We've got to go." Thomas pulled me closer to him, then held his hand out toward Andrea and Lawn. The priest gulped heavily, then took his hand, Andrea looking slightly confused but all the same, followed suit and grabbed hold of Lawn's hand.

"This will not be forgiven, Ahch!" Dolion howled as the store disappeared into burning hot flames.

CHAPTER FOURTEEN

"So . . . Who is She?"

"So that . . ." Andrea stood there with wide eyes, "that was Hell?"

"Yep," I replied flatly.

"It's almost worse the second time," Lawn mumbled. He looked a little green and dazed, but not so much so that I feared him passing out . . . again.

"I think I'm going to be sick," Andrea gagged, as she doubled over, I knelt next to her, rubbing her back. The sky above us was crystal blue and surrounding us, as far as the eye could see, was rolling green hills. We definitely didn't go to New Jersey this time. I glanced over toward Thomas, who was standing still, looking out into the distance. His face bore no expression. I patted the gagging Andrea again on the back then stood, reached out my hand, and gently touched Thomas's arm.

"Thomas?" I was going to ask him if he was okay, but his expression told me all I needed to know. So instead I asked, "Where are we?"

"A place where we might be able to find out how Dolion created the meditation room." He started to walk slowly. "And if we do, hopefully, we can find a way to destroy it."

Lawn and I shared a look. I helped Andrea stand upright and we followed after Thomas. I was never someone who liked hiking or enjoyed being outside at all, really. But even I was astonished by how pleasant this place was. Despite the bright sun, it wasn't hot, nor was it cold. And even though I couldn't see the ocean, the air carried with it the smells of the sea. But not Jersey sea air, mind you. That shit smells like old seaweed. This was much closer to a sea breeze candle scent.

"Thomas," Lawn called out. "How's your arm . . . you know, where I kind of hit you with holy water?"

I looked at the marks on his forearm, which were still really red. But they weren't blistering as they had been before.

"Oh, this." Thomas slowed his stride slightly, as he looked back at Lawn with a soft smile. "It's fine, it will heal in a few days."

"Sorry I hit you," Lawn said, frowning. "Really need to

work on my aim."

"You did great," Thomas said, shaking his head. "If anything, I should thank you . . . don't know if you noticed, but I was kind of getting my ass kicked."

"Kind of," I said, smirking.

"I'd say I had things about thirty percent under control," he said, chuckling.

After walking for about half an hour, I started to hear the soft sounds of waves crashing onto sand. A few minutes after that, we arrived at a beautiful villa, made with white sandstone, with a wide roof that provided shade for the large porch that was wrapped around it. Thick green palm trees stood tall, and behind the place was a white sand beach that led to a vibrant aqua ocean. It reminded me of a freaking postcard, maybe a laptop screen saver, not a real place.

As we reached the wide front stairs, the glass front doors opened, and from within stepped out one of the most intimidating yet strikingly beautiful women I ever had and would ever encounter. Her rich umber skin glowed with the vibrancy of youth but her dark deep-set eyes shone with wisdom that belonged to someone who had lived a long, hard life. Her ebony hair fell below her knees and glided like silk in even the slightest of breezes. Dressed in a flowing white dress, embroidered with gold trim, she looked more godlike than human.

"It's been a long time," her voice carried a somber tone, yet its forlorn melody danced pleasantly upon my ears. "What do they call you now?"

"Thomas." He walked up, greeting her with a kiss on each cheek. "Aadya, I apologize for not visiting you sooner."

"As you should," she said, with not even the slightest change to her face. Her eyes looked at the three of us, then focused on me. "She's an interesting one. A new *friend* of yours?"

Interesting? She said I was *interesting*? This gorgeous goddess finds me *interesting*!

"No," he replied, and though that's what I would have said if asked, I didn't much like him saying it. "But I like her a great deal, and if possible . . . I wanted to ask for your help on her behalf."

"Hm." She touched a delicate finger to her cheek. "I haven't seen you in almost three hundred years, and the first thing you do is ask me for a favor?"

Three hundred years, and she has skin like that? I made a mental note to ask her what skincare products she used. And to ask her for her number. Maybe to spend the rest of her life with me.

"Aadya . . . I . . ." She reached out, touched his face, causing him to fall silent instantly. Then she walked past him, stopping right in front of me. She extended her hand princess style like she wanted me to kiss it. But I wasn't about to do that, so I took it and gave her hand an awkward shake.

"Name's Riley," I introduced myself.

"I am called Aadya," Yeah, I wasn't even going to try and pronounce that. Once we got to know each other better, I would just call her "gorgeous" or something.

"Nice to meet you," I replied sheepishly, and I could literally feel the blood rushing to my face. "That's Andrea and Lawn."

"Lanh, actually," he chirped in, she offered them a soft nod in response.

"Come inside," she instructed, as she took her hand away. "There's a storm brewing."

I looked up at the clear blue sky in confusion, then followed her inside.

***

Her pad was fucking sweet. Filled with all sorts of knick knacks from around the world, decorated in lavish carpets and tapestries. It was a hippie's dream. I could spend a week looking at each object and probably wouldn't even have seen half of the shit in there. A place like this would drive Daniel nuts, he would be thinking about all the dust.

My chest let out a sad pang at the thought of Daniel.

"Your home is lovely," Andrea commented, as we entered a room lined with shelves of books. On the floor were large incredibly soft pillows to sit on, and a small low table that had an ornate tea set on its smooth surface. "Would you like us to take off our shoes? You have such lovely carpet in here, I'd hate for us to get sand on it."

"Well, I see at least one of the humans you brought with you has proper manners," she cooed. Lawn and I both looked at each other guiltily. "But that's quite alright, dear, cleaning has never been an issue for me. But of course, if you would feel more comfortable, you can remove your shoes and place them near the door."

Following Andrea's lead, we removed our shoes, then joined the goddess and Thomas on the cushions.

"So how exactly do you need my help, Thomas?"

"Dolion has somehow created a space that allows demons to enter a human's body more easily and without a contract . . . but . . . you already know this."

"Oh?" Her dark eyes watched Thomas carefully. "Do I, now?"

"That room," he said softly. "It held within it a great power. A power I couldn't imagine coming from anyone but you."

"I see." I wasn't sure what he meant, but her lips curled upward ever so slightly. "Well, you are right, I did assist Dolion in creating his . . . what did he call it, again?"

"Meditation room," Thomas replied darkly.

"Ah, yes, that's right." She ran her fingers through her hair. "What a silly name."

"Why?" Thomas shook his head. "Why did you help him?"

"Why?" She almost sounded amused . . . almost. "He

paid me, of course."

"Do you realize what could be done with that room? If he were to make more, just how many could become possessed?"

"Why should I care about that?" She raised her brow, again, only slightly. "Humans never treated my kind with the respect we deserved. Even when we healed them, taught them, protected them. How did they repay us? They hung us, drowned us, burned us at the stake. Why would I care what fate befalls them?"

"Wait! Wait, wait, wait one second!" Everyone turned to me, mostly with a look of confusion, though my beautiful goddess offered up only a cool blank stare. "You said burned at the stake?"

"Yes," she replied slowly.

"Are you a freaking witch?" I was about to jump out of my seat.

"Freaking?" She looked at Thomas. "I don't know much of the current slang, what does that mean?"

"It's a milder substitute for the Fuck, which she also uses quite often," Thomas explained. "But she isn't cursing at you. It's more or less a way to express her excitement."

"Ahh, I see," she turned back to me, slowly, narrowing a brow. "Yes, I am a witch."

"Oh my god," I practically squealed. "That's the coolest fucking thing ever."

"Indeed." She turned her attention back to Thomas. "She does curse a lot, doesn't she?"

"I think it's because she's from New Jersey."

"So you like, cast spells and stuff? Make potions, curse people? Oh! Oh, my god, can you fly on a broom?"

"I suppose I could fly on a broom if I so chose," she looked at me like I had something gross on my face. "But why would one want to do such a thing?"

"Oh, lord, I think I'm actually in love with you," I mumbled under my breath. Out of the corner of my eye, I saw Thomas frowning.

"What did you say?" The gorgeous sexy witch asked.

"Sorry," Andrea swooped in. "She was *really* obsessed with this show about witches when we were kids."

"Of course," she exhaled. "They slaughtered most of my kind, then used us to entertain children. Just another reason for me not to prevent their impending doom."

"Impending doom?" Lawn asked. "What do you mean?"

"I suppose you have yet to fully comprehend just how revolutionary what Dolion and I have created is." She sort of chuckled. "Which isn't surprising, you humans always think so small."

"Aadya," Thomas reached out and took her hands in his. "So he does intend to spread this out further? And you . . . you intend to help him?"

"Ah, my little passionflower." She stroked his hand with her thumb. "Did you really think he would be satisfied with such a small community? You know how many children they have, and they want them all on earth."

Thomas closed his eyes for a moment, took in a deep breath before opening them once more.

"Can I speak with you?" He cast a slight sideways glance in my direction. "Privately,"

"That would, perhaps, be for the best," As she stood slowly, I watched her with saddened eyes, I didn't want her to leave so soon. "Come, let's walk on the beach." She turned to us before departing."Treat my home as your own. I may not like your kind, but if Thomas deems you worthy, I have no choice but to oblige. The kitchen is just down the hall. Eat and drink what you like. And upstairs, there are extra beds, if you require rest."

What if I require you on one of those beds . . . was what I thought, but what I said was closer to a hushed thank you.

We sat there silently till we heard the front door close. Then Lawn turned to us with panic in his eyes, "I suspected Dolion wouldn't stop at one community . . . but she said impending doom?"

"¡Madre de Dios!" Andrea held her hands to her chest. "She couldn't mean the whole of humanity is doomed . . . could she?"

"She's like . . . super cool, right? Sexy as hell too. She's like, if I could, I would have her babies kind of hot." They both looked at me wide-eyed, I shrugged, "What?"

***

"I need to lie down," Andrea stood, running a hand through her wavy locks, "I hardly slept last night and all of this . . . it's too much."

We listened in silence till her footsteps faded away up the staircase. Then Lawn stood, turning to me he asked, "Want to raid the kitchen?"

"Hell, yeah!" I shot up. "Do you think she eats weird stuff? Like, eyes of newt?"

"Eye of newt?" he said, chuckling.

“Yeah, you know,” I explained. “Like in *Macbeth,* ‘Eye of newt, and toe of frog’ or whatever . . . for the potion?”

“I got the reference. But you know, eye of newt is just mustard seeds, right?"

"Is that what that is?" I frowned as we made our way to the kitchen. "That's kind of boring."

The kitchen was as awesome as the rest of the place, with a large fridge full of all sorts of fresh fruits and veggies, although unfortunately there was no meat or frozen pizza. She had a spice rack that made all others look like shit. It contained herbs I had never even heard of before. My cooking skills started and ended with putting salt and pepper on stuff and hoping for the best. Lawn started whipping up a melody of mixed vegetables. I found pasta and a pot, while I waited for the water to boil, I found her wine rack. All looked old and expensive. I popped one open and poured us two glasses.

"She probably wouldn't like me smoking inside," I said more to myself than to Lawn.

"We're already taking her food and wine, so I wouldn't."

"Well, she did say to make ourselves at home," I said, grinning.

"You can go outside. I can keep an eye on everything here," he offered.

"Nah," I waved my hand dismissively. "I can wait till after we eat." I threw the pasta in and stirred slowly. "So, how do you say her name again? Ayya? Adgya?"

"Aadya," Lawn cocked his brow. "So you care about saying her name right, but to Hell with mine?"

"Well," I said, smirking. "I'm kind of in love with her. And I just sort of like you."

"After all we've been through," he shook his head and laughed. "That hurts, Riley."

"Oh, you'll get over it," I said, laughing, but then I felt this pressure in my chest. A pressure that compelled me to ask, "Does it bother you?"

"The name thing? Riley, I was just kidding. I'm fine with it."

"Well . . . yeah, I knew you were kidding," I said, frowning. "But like . . . why are you fine with it? You. . . like . . . never called me out about pronouncing your name wrong."

"Well," he said thoughtfully, turning toward me. "When I first came to America, I didn't have much of a grip on English. I knew a few phrases but only simple things. It took time to learn and a lot of practice, and I've got to say at that time, I pronounced a lot of things . . . as well as a lot of people's names . . . wrong. And it was kind of embarrassing sometimes, especially when people made a big deal out of it."

"So you didn't want to embarrass me." I felt my cheeks flushing . . . but only slightly.

"No, I wouldn't say that." He turned back to the vegetables that were starting to smell really good. "I just don't see how making a big deal out of it helps either of us."

"Okay . . ." I said, smiling softly. "Guess that makes sense."

"Also, when I first met you," he said, flashing a toothy grin in my direction. "You were passed out on my church's steps in a nightgown telling me a ghost girl was trying to get you. I kind of thought there was a real possibility you were insane."

"Shut up." I hit him playfully. "And I wasn't wearing a "nightgown" ... you're making me sound old."

"My bad. I don't know what they're called."

"So." I took a sip of wine. "Why did you help me? If you thought I was insane and all."

"Honestly?" he smirked.

"Yeah, honestly," I pushed.

"You seemed really worried about your in-laws . . . and I thought that even if she's crazy, at least she cares about others."

"That's it?" I tilted my head to the side, as I watched him take the pan off the flames.

"I think a lot of people would see something like you did and just run home. But you ran to get help, and it was for them. That's why I helped."

"I'm surprised," I said, chuckling. "You're pretty easy."

"Well," the right corner of his mouth lifted as he spoke. "It also helped that you're pretty cute."

"Y-you," I stammered, as my cheeks went from pink to ruby. "You're a horrible priest!"

"You think?" he laughed.

"Yeah, like really bad," I turned my attention back to the pasta. "You should change careers."

"Hm," I felt his eyes on the back of my neck. "After all of this, maybe I could be a professional demon hunter."

"Oh, yeah?" I challenged. "One that passes out all the time?"

"Hey, I was pretty badass in the Dollar Store." He made a gun with his hands and gestured like he was shooting. "You have to admit that."

"Yeah, after you woke up." I rolled my eyes.

"Didn't pass out that time," he said defensively. "That Dolion guy hit me over the head."

"He did?" I turned around fast. "Are you okay?"

"I'm fine!"

I reached out and touched the back of his head.

He winced, grabbing my hand, pulling it from his head injury. "Less fine when you poke at it like that."

"Sorry," I mumbled. We were a bit too close, and now he was holding my hand. Despite all the hell transporting and demon-fighting, he somehow smelled really . . . really fucking good. And the worst part was that I had put us in that position. And I was married . . . technically. And he was a priest. And he thought I was . . . cute.

"You don't have to keep holding my hand," I said, as I tried desperately not to get lost in his deep eyes.

"Yeah . . . I don't," he agreed, though he didn't let go.

"The pasta's probably over-cooked," I murmured. "I should go check it."

"Yeah . . . that would be a good idea." But neither of us made a move to step away, in fact, we might have gotten a bit closer.

"You really are a horrible priest."

"You know what," he smiled as he closed the space between us even further. "You might be right."

I felt like shit, but I also wanted to kiss him. But I thought about Daniel . . . even if he was a demon now . . . he wasn't technically dead. And sure, he had basically sold my soul to demons without my consent, which was a total dick move. And for sure, I was going to divorce the shit out of him if I ever managed to get him unpossessed. But still . . . as of that moment, I was still a married lady.

Furthermore . . . there was Andrea. I gave her a hard time about flirting with Lawn and yet here I was about to make out with him? *Now that was a dick move on my part.* Not only girl code, but my own weird sense of morals would dictate that I not kiss him. But his lips looked so inviting.

But before I could make up my mind . . .

"Knock, knock." We jumped, looking toward the voice, a pit formed in my stomach. It was Daniel . . . But it most definitely wasn't him. There was this sly smile on his face that distorted his features in a way that made him look like another person entirely. "Am I interrupting?"

He glided toward us, his movements fluid and cat-like. Lawn moved in front of me, grabbed the knife he had been using. Together we backed away, trying to keep some distance between us and my demon-possessed husband.

"Riley, I have to say, I'm disappointed," Other Daniel cooed. "After so many years of loyalty and commitment, and now I find you like this, and with a priest no less..."

"W-we weren't, I mean . . . wait a second." I stammered. "Stop talking like you're Daniel, I know you're not!"

"Very perceptive." Other Daniel giggled, moving closer, Lawn held the knife up toward his . . . its . . . throat, "you should put that down, dearie, before you hurt yourself ... or I hurt you."

At the entrance to the kitchen, Dolion appeared with Andrea, her eyes spaced out, almost like she was under a spell. I tugged on Lawn's arm and gestured toward Andrea. He nodded, but we were cornered, and there really wasn't anything we could do. We needed Thomas.

"Riley." Dolion moved closer, his hand firmly on Andrea's shoulder. "Why do you insist on making this all so difficult?"

"Why do you insist on being a complete and total fucktard?" I snapped.

"Oh, she is feisty!" Other Daniel clasped his hands together. "Though if I had to pick, I prefer her friend here. She's just scrumptious."

"Take her." Dolion passed her off like she was a fucking rag doll. "Though Erica will be disappointed. She also fancied this one."

"I normally wouldn't mind sharing." Other Daniel cupped her face in his hand. "But it's so hard to find someone this pure . . . I can't wait to make her filthy."

"Get your fucking hands off her!" I almost charged forward but Lawn held me back, which was a good thing because I'd already tackled one demon today and she was way smaller than Daniel and that had already hurt like a bitch.

"Isn't that just so sweet? You have so much love for this human. But do you know how much your devoted husband lusted after this one?" Other Daniel chuckled. "He would pleasure himself with the thought of her quite frequently. Even once when he was making love to you, he. . ."

"Okay, okay, ew!" I interrupted. "First off, everyone has fantasies and it's fucking rude for you to be sharing his all willy nilly like that! And two . . . of course he fantasized about Andrea! She's sexy as hell! If she weren't like family to me and we hadn't known each other since, like, forever, I'd probably jerk off to her sometimes as well! So, stop being nasty, and mind your own damn business! Also, can someone turn off the stove? The pasta's totally mush now and I don't want to burn down the sexy witch lady's kitchen."

"My, oh, my." Other Daniel pulled Andrea even closer to him, making my blood boil. "I'm starting to see why Thomas likes you so much."

"Really?" Dolion asked, his voice filled with cold disdain. He walked past Other Daniel, turned off the stove, then looked at me with those flat black eyes. "More and more I find myself wondering why both Thomas and *she* are so enamored by someone as crass and insignificant as her."

Honestly, I had nothing to say to that. I had wondered the same thing many times.

"Dolion," I spoke slowly this time, carefully. "If I go with you . . . will you let Andrea and Lawn go?"

"Riley!" Lawn began to protest, but I pinched his arm to shut him up.

"I'm afraid we are long past such negotiation, Riley." He grabbed Lawn's hand with lighting speed and twisted it till he dropped the knife. Lawn let out a cry of pain as Dolion forced him to his knees. "You've been an annoyance, one that will be put to bed soon."

"Dolion, stop!" It was Thomas.

Thank God! Well . . . not God . . .

"Aadya," Dolion glared, releasing Lawn. I bent down to his side, checked his wrist that had already begun to turn black and blue. "I thought I told you to keep him busy?"

Dang it . . . hot witch betrayed us.

"I'm not one of your minions," Aadya fired back coolly. "Besides, I took him away from here for a while. It isn't my fault you took so long."

Even though she betrayed us . . . I couldn't help but think she was still so fucking cool.

"Why are you doing all of this?" Thomas moved cautiously toward Dolion. But he stopped suddenly, still staring at Other Daniel. "You?"

"Surprise," Other Daniel cooed. "It's been a while, hasn't it?"

"What are you doing here?" Thomas demanded. "And in . . . that body?"

"I know, I know," Other Daniel chuckled. "Not my usual type, but *she* thought it would be funny and I agreed."

"Dolion," Thomas growled. "You're not one to play games like this. Is this for *her*?"

"For us!" he snapped. "For all of us! These greedy humans are a plague on this planet. All they do is take, while we feed off their scraps or burn in the fires of Hell. It's time we take it! We are older than them, and wiser. This planet should be ours."

"This isn't our way." Thomas shook his head.

"No," Dolion smiled in true villain style. "But it will be."

Just then, Aadya touched the back of Thomas' neck, and a strange glowing circle formed. He let out a cry as he crumbled to the ground. His whole body was encompassed by the glowing circle. He struggled, trying to move, but the glow wouldn't let him. His eyes turned to the beautiful witch. "Aadya . . . why?"

"I'm sorry, my little passionflower," she said in a way that made me think she meant it. "It may take time ... but you will see this is all for the best."

Just when I was thinking about how totally and completely fucked we were, I felt Lawn grabbing my hand. He looked at me, his face twisted in pain, then he gestured his head toward the kitchen's entrance and mouthed, *Water gun . . . sitting room.* Then he leapt up, tackling Dolion, who hardly moved, but it gave me enough room to get out of there quickly. I ran to the sitting room, and next to the cushion, there was the water gun. I grabbed it, and though nearly empty, it was something.

I ran back out into the hall. Dolion had followed me from the kitchen and was approaching swiftly. Before he could grab me, I squirted water straight into his face. He let out a ferocious cry as I ran past him and into the kitchen. I squirted Other Daniel in the face. He freaked, letting go of Andrea. I grasped hold of her, but Dolion appeared suddenly and grabbed the back of my neck. He tossed me across the floor and I crashed into the spellbound Thomas.

"Take that human now!" Dolion barked at Other Daniel, who despite his sizzling face, obliged and went to grab hold of Andrea once more. Lawn leaped forward. Trying to intercept, but in one fiery instant, all three of them vanished.

"Fuck!" I screamed; my heart sinking to the bottom of my stomach. I turned to Dolion, keeping the nearly empty water gun pointed at him. "Bring them back!"

"And why would I do that?" Dolion said, cackling.. "How much of that water do you have left, Riley? Do you think it's enough to actually stop me? Are you that foolish?" He approached me, slowly, clearly in a lot of pain. I held up the water gun, then I felt Thomas wrapping his arms around me. The glow, whatever it was, tingled against my body, almost like static electricity.

"Dolion . . ." Thomas' every word carried with it a pain-filled weight. "Just give me her . . . just her. I don't care about the others. I don't care about the rest of the people on this planet, just Riley. And I promise I will never go against you or *her* again."

That forced Dolion to stop, and me to make a weird noise between a '*Huh*' and a '*What?*'.

"And you . . . would you rejoin us?" His voice was soft, almost fearful. In two seconds flat, Dolion had gone from fucking psycho killer to a soft marshmallow.

"If that's what it takes," Thomas relented. "If coming back for good will spare her . . . I'll do that."

"I will . . . have to speak with *her.* But perhaps we can come to some agreement." Dolion glanced at Aadya. "Release him."

"Only if you ask nicely," she replied. "Remember, I am not one of your minions."

"Aadya, if you would be so kind?" Dolion sounded almost too composed.

"Very well." With a wave of her hand, the glow vanished and Thomas's whole body seemed to relax on top of me. It was a bit heavy, to be honest.

"I will go and discuss this matter with her." Dolion peered at Thomas. "Stay here and recover while I do." And with a sudden burst of flame, he was gone, leaving me, Thomas, and the sexy witch in a truly awkward and extremely uncomfortable silence.

Finally, the witch lady broke the silence by walking over to the stove, taking the pot and draining the water within. I slowly helped Thomas off me and leaned him against the wall. He was trembling terribly, and his skin was as cold as ice.

"Do you have blankets?" I asked her.

She turned with a click of her tongue."Of course I do." She took a wine glass out and poured herself a glass from the open bottle. "But that won't help him. Just give him a few minutes and his core temperature will regulate itself."

"A blanket wouldn't hurt, though." He let out the saddest excuse for a chuckle I had ever heard.

"Well, I'm not getting it for you." She poured herself wine from the bottle I had opened and took a delicate sip. "You brought this all on yourself, my little passionflower. You know I don't like hurting you, but you left me little choice."

"Could have used a slightly weaker binding spell," he said, grinning.

"Well." She took another sip. "I could have . . . but I am still upset that you haven't visited me in so long."

"That's fair," he groaned.

"You know, *she* isn't as gullible as Dolion," she said, with a sigh. "*She* won't believe you will give up your freedom for just one human."

"I know," he replied. "But it gives me some time to think of a new plan."

"I won't help you."

"Yeah," he said, with a sigh. "I know that now."

Silence followed as I looked back and forth between them. The tension in the air was so thick, I almost choked.

There was a lot of history here, *clearly.* A history that for sure wasn't my business. I was just happy to hear Thomas had been lying to Dolion, because that meant he might help me save Andrea and Lawn . . . no, I *knew* it meant he would.

"But I won't stop you either." She poured herself more wine, then sauntered out of the room. "I'll leave the two of you to talk. I'm sure you have much to discuss."

"Riley?" He looked at me with those sad puppy dog eyes. "I'm sorry I brought you here that I failed to protect your friends. But . . . I have an idea on how to get them back. Aadya wouldn't tell me much, but she told me enough to put an end to the meditation room . . . hopefully."

"Okay," I said, nodding slowly. "But, hey, listen . . . don't apologize. Like, you've really saved us – over and over. You're allowed to make one bad call. I am worried about Andrea though . . . they had her under some kind of trance . . ."

"Don't worry." He shook his head, then reached out to touch the side of my face. "To take someone as pure as her would take a long time . . . as long as she doesn't go into the meditation room. But trust me, I will recover soon, and I will get her. I promise."

"And Lawn?" I reminded him.

"Yeah, I guess I can get him too," he said, chuckling, but that quickly turned into a coughing fit. I let his breathing return to normal before I spoke again.

"There's something I've wanted to talk to you about for a while . . ." I started slowly. "But I didn't want to push or stick my nose where it doesn't belong. But I think it's kind of important that I'm more in the know."

"Okay?" he said, furrowing his brow.

"So . . . who is *she*?"

"All right," he said, with a sigh. "Help me up. I'll tell you everything. But let's go outside . . . I need a smoke."

CHAPTER FIFTEEN

I've Got Everything Under Control

"It's . . ." Was all he managed to say after an annoyingly long silence.

"Complicated," I offered him some assistance.

"Yeah . . ." He scratched the back of his head.

"So why don't we start with something . . . simpler?" I suggested. "The demon inside Daniel . . . you seemed surprised to see it?"

"You could say that she . . . well . . . she usually takes female hosts."

"Okay." I slowly took in the sunset dipped waves crashing onto the smooth sand below, admiring their beauty, not for the first time. "So, do demons have genders themselves?

Like people do?"

"Yes and no," Thomas took in a long drag, "We're not created with any specific gender, but among those of us who possess humans, some form preferences."

"Do you have a preference?" I asked.

"Not really," he replied. "I go both ways."

"But this demon in Daniel . . . likes to be a woman . . . so, why is she in Daniel? She said for fun?"

"Yeah." As he spoke, smoke billowed out from between his lips. "That's where we start getting complicated."

"If I had to take a wild and crazy guess . . . I would say you two have history."

"That's one way of putting it." He shook his head. "It's been years . . . she never really got over it."

"So demons, like . . . date? Get married, and shit like that?" It was weird to imagine fiery Hell, people getting tortured, and demons going out for a night on the town.

"We form connections, some of us. Some of these connections are fleeting, some of them last a long time . . . some last through all eternity. But it's not like humans. We don't love, Riley, not like you do. But being alive for as long as we are, it gets . . . lonely."

"I get that." I flashed him a crooked smile. "I hate most people, and I love being alone . . . yet . . . I get lonely all the time. And honestly? Yeah, it's gotten worse as I've gotten older, and I'm only twenty-eight. I can't even imagine how you feel."

"Riley." He looked at me with a soft smile. "I want you to remember it's different. My feeling lonely . . . and yours . . . My emotions aren't like yours. It's so . . . difficult to explain. This . . . this is why I don't like talking about these things with humans. Your species is so prone to sympathy. I don't want you to think I'm like you, that my kind is like you. We were created to enlist pain and suffering, you cannot forget that."

"I know, I know," I said, rolling my eyes. "You're a big scary demon. I should tremble before you."

"Riley . . ."

"Okay, listen, I get that you're different." I held up my hand. "Don't get it twisted. I still think it's all shades of fucked up that you are all taking people's bodies, using them all as you please and sending people's souls to Hell. Like if you weren't helping me so much, trust me when I say, I would be trying to get you out of that poor guy's body just like I am trying to do for everyone in Lilith's Gardens. Hell, when this is all over, I just might."

"Alright," he said, chuckling. "That's good."

"And it will be super easy because I know your name," I added with a sly smirk.

"That may be true," he said, winking. "But I could always find another body and come right back to bother you."

"And then I'll send you away again," I countered. "Over and over again till either you get bored or I die."

"Is it weird that I kind of like the sound of that?" he said, chuckling.

"No, that's very in keeping with your character." I shook my head. "You're kind of a masochist."

"You know you're not the first person who's told me that."

"Not surprised." Our laughter faded into the sea breeze. I let the moment linger, just for a bit. I knew we were in crunch time, that I had to hurry and get Andrea and Lawn back. But honestly, a part of me thought it would likely be the last time I saw the ocean. The last time I would smoke a cigarette with someone, and the last time I would enjoy a sunset.

"Kind of sucks that your ex is now in the body of my soon-to-be-ex," I mumbled.

"That's why they did it, Because it would make things more difficult for us."

"Dick move."

"Tell me about it."

"Okay." I took in a breath. "That was the warm-up round, now let's get to the tough stuff."

He nodded.

"You and Dolion . . . you're close too."

"Not close like how I am with the demon inside of Daniel," he clarified. "But we have known one another all our lives."

"He said family," I pushed.

"A very human thing for him to say." Thomas sighed as

he lit up another cigarette. "But if you were to try and compare what we are to a relationship between humans . . . I suppose one would consider us brothers."

"Is that what that name he always calls you . . . achoo or whatever means? Brother?"

"Ahch," he said, nodding. "Yes, that's what it means. But we're not brothers in the same way humans would be brothers. Though we were created by the same entity . . . we were both created by *her*."

"*Her* as in the demon that wants my body, yeah?"

He nodded slowly.

"And she's the one I saw at my in-laws place and in the bathroom?

He nodded again.

"So is that like . . . that's how demons really look?" I asked, mentally trying to convert an image of Thomas looking like a Japanese ghost. For some reason, the thought was more humorous than scary.

"No," Thomas said softly. "I'm not sure how she appeared to you exactly, but it's most likely that the form she chose was something she knew would scare you."

"Oh," I let out a sarcastic chuckle. "So that was custom tailored for me? I'm flattered."

"Lillith always enjoyed . . . tormenting her victims."

"And I thought It was bad that my mom was distant." I took a long drag. "But I'd take that over a crazy lady that likes torturing people."

"Again," Thomas reiterated. "She may have created me, but she's not my "mother."

"Right," I said, nodding as I tried to digest this information. "Because demons aren't born like humans are?"

"No, we are not. Most demons do not have reproductive organs. So such a thing wouldn't be possible . . . most of the time."

"Most of the time?" I raised my brow.

"There are one or two exceptions to that . . . *she* is actually one of them."

"But you said *she* made you in a non-vaginal kind of way."

"Yes, she created us the old-fashioned way," Thomas took another drag, "But from there ... it was different."

"Oh," My eyes widened. "So she, like, made you and Dolion so that you could, like. . . go to pound town . . . in the human sense?"

"Yes." He twisted his cigarette between his fingertips. "But I was never . . . how do I say this . . . I was never interested. Dolion, on the other hand . . . They have been a pair for some time."

"That's what sexy witch meant when she said they had all those children!"

"Out of all the demon clans, theirs is the largest." His voice was distant. "Creating demons the old fashioned way takes time and energy. She went against that natural order."

"So . . . Dolion and you are like her kids? But she made you to . . . help her make more kids?" I couldn't stop the look of disgust from forming on my face.

"To a human, I'm sure that sounds gross," he said, chuckling. "But again, trust me, though she made us, it was nothing close to how humans give birth."

"Still, it's kind of weird." I might have been being judgmental, but I had never been a fan of incest. I stopped watching *Game of Thrones* the minute I saw the brother and sister in bed together. I also loved John Irving novels but couldn't finish *The Hotel New Hampshire* for the same reason. . . Yuck.

"To a human, yes . . . to demons, it's normal," he said, shrugging.

"But you weren't into it?" I asked.

"Much to *her* annoyance, no. "I had no desire to sire children of my own . . . But we never saw eye to eye on anything really. I'm a bit of a black sheep within my clan, which became worse when I started befriending humans, and only taking over human bodies for short periods of time. Even my relationship with the demon that now resides inside Daniel. She's from another clan . . . such fraternizations are not common practice in Hell."

"So you're a straight-up rebel, huh?"

"My clan would more likely be prone to using the word annoyance . . . perhaps now, traitor . . . but yes."

"So does every clan possess people as much as yours?" I

asked.

"No, well, not that it doesn't happen at all. But most other demon clans remain in the domains assigned to them." He shook his head. "But *she* . . . *she* is different. From the beginning, *she* has been obsessed with getting back to earth."

"Getting . . . back?"

"Yes. . ." He looked at me with distant eyes. "*She* isn't like the other demons . . . *she* once was something much different. A long time ago . . . back when her name was Lilith."

"*She* was . . . human?"

"Yes, one of the first." He looked off into the distance.

"How does a human become a demon?"

"Through terrible . . . monstrous acts." He took a long drag that turned the rest of his cigarette to ash. "Worse than anything you could possibly imagine."

"And now *she* wants to take over my body?" I remembered her that first night, her long dark hair, grotesque skin, those pitch-black eyes, and a chill passed through me.

"Yes, but not only you . . . *she* wants every one of her children here on earth." He closed his eyes. "And now . . . she might have found a way to do it."

"But we can stop *her,* right?" I reached out, touching his hand gingerly. "What did the sexy witch say?"

"There's a possibility," he murmured. "But it's slim . . . almost impossible, and can only be done from within the room . . . I'm sorry, Riley. If I had realized what they were doing . . . I never would have participated. I thought this was just another one of Dolion's plans that would ultimately fail. He's had so many stupid ideas. But I never thought he would go to a witch for help . . . even further, I never would have expected him to go to Aadya . . ."

"Hey, don't be so hard on yourself." I patted his back. "Sure, there was a plan to doom all of humanity brewing right under your nose and you had no idea. But you are a demon, you have no obligation to help us. Honestly, still not sure why you are . . . though, trust me, I'm not complaining."

"If they all come here . . . then earth will be just as bad as Hell," he said, adding a sigh for good measure. "And for all their flaws, for all the bad they do, I still enjoy humans. Their complex natures, how they can be greedy, and yet selfless, both kind and cruel. Humans can surprise me, challenge me. Demons...we are just selfish. Purely, simply."

"Honestly, I've always thought people were super selfish. But you've been around longer than I have so, who knows? Maybe you see something I don't."

"You say that, yet you still want to go headfirst into danger and save all the people at Lilith's Gardens."

"Well, I want to save Andrea and Lawn . . . Daniel and his parents too, I guess . . . if that's even possible." I shrugged. "And if I just so happen to save the others as well . . . I mean, I wouldn't be mad about it."

"Riley . . ." He turned to me with a wide smile, his eyes practically shimmering. "I truly like you. So much so, that it continues to astonish me."

"Urgh." I rolled my eyes. "For a big scary demon, you're awfully sappy."

"Aadya tells me that quite often as well."

"Okay! One last hard-hitting question before we go and save our comrades and maybe a bunch of other people I care less about . . ."

"If it's concerning Aadya, I want to say flat out that there's nothing even close to romance between us."

"Oh no," I said, with a smirk. "Wasn't going to ask that. She's way out of your league."

"Thanks," he said, laughing.

"No, my question is . . . what's with the whole 'my little passionflower' thing?"

"Oh, that." He looked away with clear embarrassment on his face. "It's just a nickname."

"And?"

"And what?"

"What does it mean?"

"You wouldn't understand, it's a private thing." His face was growing red.

"Are you blushing?" My smile was so sharp, it could cut cheddar. "You have to tell me now!"

"Riley."

"Oh, come on. I could make you tell me."

"You could," he agreed, "But you won't."

"Okay, fine, I won't," I laughed. "But don't you like me?"

"Riley, that's not fair."

"If you like me as much as you say you do, you will tell me."

"Fine," he relented. "It's a little bit embarrassing."

"I'm kind of hoping it's a lot embarrassing . . . but please, continue."

"The passion flower or passiflora mixta is a flower that grows near volcanoes," he explained while not even trying to look me in the eye. "She calls me that because . . . to her, they show that beautiful things can come from even the most volatile and dangerous places."

"Oh my." I couldn't contain it, I full-on cracked up. "That's so cute."

"It's not . . . whatever." He turned a shade redder. "Let's go save your friends and stupid husband . . . okay?"

"Alright, just give me a minute!" I wheezed. "My side hurts . . . "

***

"So you're leaving?" Aadya asked, as she approached us coolly.

"Yes," Thomas said, nodding. "And despite everything that happened . . . I wanted to say goodbye properly."

"You had better," she half-smiled, opening her arms to him. "Otherwise, I would have had to put a curse on you."

He chuckled as he wrapped her in a tight embrace. "I don't like when we're not on the same side."

"My sweet passionflower," she murmured. "You should know by now, I'm on no one's side but my own."

Damn, she was so cool.

"Human." She turned to me. "To you, I will extend a courteous apology for the trouble. More because I care for Thomas than because I actually feel any regret."

"Hell, I'll take that," I said, suddenly beaming.

"Come." She opened her arms, offering me a hug that I half-ran into out of pure excitement. I still hated hugs . . . but I mean she was the embodiment of perfection and smelled like honey and lavender, so I wasn't about to pass that up. As she wrapped her arms around me, she whispered in my ear, "Even though I assisted in that meditation room's creation, there's no way of knowing what will occur if it is destroyed. So, human, I want you to promise me . . . to ensure that Thomas is nowhere near that place, if you succeed."

"I promise," I whispered back, taking in her scent once more before the most incredible hug of my life ended. "I kind of planned on not having him be there."

The embrace ended with a soft nod from Aadya and I

walked over to Thomas, holding out my hand. He smiled and took it, then pulled me in closer. I looked back at Aadya; her face was as stoic as ever, but if you looked closely enough, you could see the slight furl of her brow, the concern in her deep-set eyes.

"Don't worry,"As a dreadful heat began to surround me, I called out to her. "I've got everything under control!"

And with that, we were gone.

CHAPTER SIXTEEN

You Know How In-laws Can Be

We materialized in Dolion's mansion entrance, but it was unlike every other time I had seen it – full of light and demon people dancing and laughing. Now the place was dark . . . and honestly, ridiculously creepy. I looked at Thomas with wide eyes – I hadn't expected him to bring us right into the action.

I didn't even know what the plan was, really, and I was starting to feel like an idiot for not asking before we left. Still holding my hand, he brought me up the stairwell. The whole place was dead silent, except for the sound of our footsteps. At the top of the stairs, Thomas stopped and closed his eyes.

"What are you doing?" I whispered.

"Trying to determine where Andrea and Lanh are," he

explained in a hushed tone.

"How?"

"Tracking their essence." He opened his eyes. "They should be down this way." He guided me down the hall to the right . . . away from the meditation room. I glanced around, trying to listen for even the most subtle noise. But there was nothing. I focused on Thomas. His face was serious, his steps cautious.

"Can you, like, sense the other demons too?" I asked.

He nodded slowly, his golden watching my reactions.

"So they can sense us as well," I gulped down hard, not really wanting to hear the answer.

"Yes." He nodded again.

"And what is the plan . . . how are we destroying the meditation room?"

"Not we," he replied. "After we get your friends . . . you will take them and leave. I will handle the meditation room."

"Um . . . okay." *Fuck!* That was so not what I wanted to hear. I thought about protesting, but his face told me that he had made up his mind, "But how are you going to do that? Like what did the sexy witch tell you?"

"Riley." He looked at me. "I'll handle it . . . trust me."

"I still want to know what the plan is," I insisted.

"What did Aadya whisper to you?" he countered.

"Nothing really," I lied. "She just told me to try not to die because you would be sad if I did."

He studied my face for a moment and my heart rate spiked. I knew he could see people's sins,, but I really hoped he could see that I just kind of fibbed. *Were such small lies sin worthy?* After a moment, he shook his head. "Let's just focus on getting Andrea and Lanh back . . . now's not the best time to be arguing."

As true as that was . . . I still didn't know how he was planning to destroy the room, which would be a problem for the plan I was concocting in my head. But I decided to not push my luck, and as he said, focus on the immediate task at hand. We made our way down the hall until we reached the second to last room. Thomas gestured to the door, gave me a small nod, then busted it open.

The room was incredibly bare bones. The walls were jade green, the floor a deep oak, and at the room's center was a luxurious love seat that faced the door with a single light above it, illuminating the figure upon it. *Andrea.* She was seated there, her eyes glazed over like they had been back at the beach villa. I had to stop myself from running in and tackling her. I mean, this was so unbelievably, obviously, a trap. Like they weren't even trying to hide it, which made me think . . .

"Hello," a voice whispered into my ear. I let out a yelp and tripped over the door frame, landing square on my ass. A shock wave ran up my tail bone. Other Daniel looked down at me and chuckled coldly before turning his attention to Thomas. "I'm surprised you came so soon. You didn't even give us time to ready the celebration." Other Daniel walked around me and stood behind Andrea, placing one hand on her shoulder and the other on the back of the love seat.

I moved to my feet with a little assistance from Thomas and glared at Other Daniel more than I had ever glared at anyone before.

"Why come here?" Thomas asked Other Daniel. "Are you really planning to help them?"

"Darlin', I don't know why you're surprised." Other Daniel moved the hand on Andrea's shoulder to her hair, stroking it gently. "Dolion's little take-over-earth schemes may have been silly in the past. But this?! How could I pass it up? With his little meditation room, I can have anybody I want. Including *this one*."

"You won't take her. I won't let you!"

"And how do you plan to stop me?" Other Daniel laughed. "You know, when we take over a person's body, we gain access to everything about them, all their memories, everything. I know you, Riley. I know what you are capable of, and trust me, it's not much."

"Stop this," Thomas warned. "Let me have the girl . . . and the priest. You don't want to fight me. It will not work in your favor."

"Would you really fight me, darling?" Other Daniel giggled, which was really fucking weird. Also, it was strange hearing his voice calling a guy darling, even if it wasn't really him speaking. "After everything we've been through?"

"I don't wish to." Thomas murmured. "But if I must . . . I will."

"All for that human?" Other Daniel chuckled as he twirled a strand of Andrea's hair between his fingers. "You've really changed. I remember all the fun we used to have. All the chaos we caused. It's pitiful how boring you've become."

"Boring's better than being a creepy asshole like you."

"Riley . . . You think I'm boring?" Thomas looked at me with sad puppy eyes, while Other Daniel giggled irritatingly.

"What? No . . ." *Was he really asking me that right now?* "I was just trying to say you're better than that creepy version of my soon to be ex-husband. Don't take everything so personally."

"So . . . you don't think I'm boring?"

"Thomas, focus!" I snapped.

"Oh, my," Other Daniel said, smirking. "Humans are even ordering you about now? How pathetic."

"Shut up, you!" My nostrils flared. "And stop touching her like that."

"If you think this is bad, just wait," Other Daniel grabbed her face, giving it a rough squeeze. "I wish I could show you all the things I will do to her, it's a shame you will be long gone by then. Oh, how I can't wait to exploit her every weakness, divulge her every secret. Well, I suppose I could do that now. It would be much more fun to tell her closest friend that she . . ."

"Enough!" Thomas leaped from my side and in seconds was holding Other Daniel up by his neck. "I will be taking the humans. Try and stop me, and I will kill you."

I took the opportunity to run to Andrea. I made one small attempt to pick her up, but my spaghetti arms could barely budge her. Not that she was heavy by any means, but I was weak. Like a ten-pound weight was a lot for me kind of weak.

"Kill me?" Other Daniel laughed viciously. "Kill this body, maybe, but me? Not even you are that much of a traitor."

So demons could be killed? Like permanently? That was interesting.

"Don't push me," Thomas said through gritted teeth.

"Fine, fine," Other Daniel said, like it was no big deal. "Can you put me down? You can take the humans for now. What do I care? You think you can actually stop Dolion? Please. If I can't have them, I can just get them later. After you completely and utterly fail."

Thomas placed Other Daniel back on the ground. "So . . . you will let us take the humans?"

"For now." Other Daniel reached out to touch Thomas's face, but he moved out of the way. "Dolion doesn't care about them, he wants you and Riley. I was told to take you to the meditation room but . . . I have a feeling you will go there anyway."

Other Daniel turned on her heels and walked toward the door.

"Wait, where's Lawn?" I implored.

"The priest?" Other Daniel said, chuckling. "Poor thing's passed out on the floor over there."

I followed Other Daniel's finger and saw Lawn crumpled up in the corner, looking close to death. Of course, he would have passed out again. I should have really expected it this time.

"I hardly did anything to the poor creature and he went out like a light," Other Daniel sneered. "Him, I won't be coming back for. Much too boring. I'll let one of the other demons have him. But not her, trust me ... I will return for that pretty young thing eventually. But for now, I bid you adieu."

And with a quick burst of flames Other Daniel was gone, and so was the chance of me saving my soon to be ex-husband. . . maybe. We would have to see how this all went. I watched Thomas slowly crossing the room and picking up Lawn with ease. I stood up and helped Thomas place him down next to Andrea.

"Will she be okay?" I asked.

"She's under a trance right now," Thomas explained. "It should fade in a few hours."

"Okay," I said, sighing with relief. "That's good."

"Sorry," Thomas' voice was somber. "I shouldn't have let Other Daniel . . . it's just . . ."

"Complicated." I touched his shoulder gently. "I get it. We'll worry about that later . . . if there is a later."

"There will be." Thomas clasped his hand on my shoulder, giving it a light squeeze. "I won't let Dolion succeed... but first, let's get these two out of here."

"No," I said, shaking my head.

"What do you mean, no?" He turned to look at me, but before he could say another word, I spoke his name and asked, "How can the meditation room be destroyed?"

"In the room, there is an altar, and on top of it is an old box. Within, there is a bewitched object; that object is what gives the room its power. The only way the room could be destroyed is if that object is eliminated." He had answered me quickly, mechanically, as if he were compelled to do so. But as soon as he finished his face twisted in concern. "Riley, why did you . . ."

I spoke his true name once more, then before I could change my mind, I instructed, "You will leave me here, take Andrea and Lawn to my apartment and never return to Lilith's Gardens ever again."

"Riley." His jaw clenched. "What have you done?"

"I know you don't feel the same way I do. I know you're a big scary demon and all . . . but I also know you don't want to go against Dolion. I know you care about him." I took in a shaky breath, ignoring the water forming in my eyes. "You can try to play it off, but I know he matters to you. So, I can't let you fight him, not for me."

"Do you realize how insanely bad of an idea this is?" I didn't know if it was a trick of the light, but I swore I saw tears forming in his eyes. "If you go into that room . . ."

"I know." I swallowed down the knot that was forming in my throat, then before I could stop myself, I wrapped my arms around his neck and hugged him tightly. "I know I'm opening myself up to them. I know this probably won't work. But this is my plan . . . It's not a good plan . . . but it's what I'm doing. . . alright?

"Alright." He nuzzled his face into my neck, and I swore I almost burst into tears.

"But if I totally mess this up..." I pulled away enough to look him straight in the eye. "You'll visit me, right?"

"All the time." He touched my cheek, collecting the tears that had fallen out against my will. "So much so, that you'll get sick of me."

"Good," I half-laughed-half sobbed. "Now get out of here, don't make me invoke your name again."

Thomas tucked Lawn under his arm, then picked up Andrea delicately, before turning to me once more. I took that moment to look at all three of them. Andrea; my friend, my family, the one person in the world who had always been there for me no matter what. Lawn, who despite being prone to fainting spells, was still the coolest priest I had ever met. And Thomas, the demon, who winked *way* too much, and yet . . . damn, I was going to miss them all if I fucked this up.

"Goodbye," I murmured. "Keep them safe . . . okay?"

"Till we meet again," he said, casting me a wink, as white-hot flames surrounded them, taking them far away. Leaving me in that room . . . that mansion . . . filled with a bunch of fucking demons . . . completely and totally alone.

Well . . . Fuck.

***

I was standing right in front of those obnoxious golden doors, about ready to pee my pants. Like, I really should have used the bathroom on my way there. I knew where it was but I had walked right past it. But nope, I went right to the meditation room and now Dolion was there, staring at me with anger filled black eyes. All I could think to do was give him a small little wave and say, "Hey." My voice cracked a little. "How's it going?"

"You sent Thomas away?" His voice boomed like thunder, and I was a little ashamed to say, there might have been a slight trickle of pee that escaped into my underpants.

"Oh . . . yeah, sorry about that." I tried to smile but it appeared as more of a grimace. "You know, with you guys being family and all . . . just didn't want to involve him in this . . ."

"You foolish, small-minded wench," he growled. The insults might have continued but then the doors slowly opened, distracting him for a moment. I felt my knees knocking against each other. Dolion looked back at me, but he was much more composed. "No matter . . . we will be done with you soon enough."

He stepped aside, gesturing for me to enter the room.

"After you."

"How kind of you," I muttered under my breath. I took a step forward, but a sudden burst of cold caused me to stop in my tracks.

"What's wrong?" he asked mockingly. "Isn't this what you came here for? To destroy this very room? Well, it's right there, open and waiting. Just for you, so why hesitate?"

"Not hesitating, just was kind of thinking I might need a bathroom break first."

He looked at me like I was the most disgusting thing he had ever heard.

"Okay, no bathroom break," I walked slowly into the deep black void before me. "But if I pee in there, it's not my fault." It was like stepping into an ice bath. Or maybe it was worse – I don't know, I had never taken an ice bath. The minute I entered, it was like my fingers and toes decided to high-tail it off my body, that was how fucking numb they were. And with every step, it spread further, till it felt like my body no longer existed, like I had become one with the darkness around me.

Then I heard *her, it's, Lilith's* voice. But this time, it didn't start as a soft hum. No, it was like she was standing next to me... or ... within me.

"I am so happy you have come back, Riley," she purred.

I tried to keep moving, searching through the darkness. But I couldn't see anything. No altar, no box – nothing. But it had to be there.

"All your wildest dreams will be a reality, Riley," she continued. *"People everywhere will finally read your words, and they will love them. They will love you."*

I tried to tune her out, but it seemed like she was literally becoming a part of my brain, so that wasn't going to work. Last time, Thomas had warned me not to engage with her. But would that really matter now? My mind was open and she was deep in there. But she didn't have complete control, not yet anyway.

"Yeah, I think you need to recalibrate your manipulation tactics," I snapped back, squinting in the darkness. "I don't care about people loving me or not."

"Oh, Riley," she cooed. *"Of course you do. All you ever really wanted was to be loved by your family, your peers, but most of all, your mother."*

"How about we don't talk about my mommy issues," I groaned. This cold darkness was getting harder and harder to wade through. But in the distance . . .I thought I could make out something.

"She was never there for you," the bitch continued. *"Never. The one person who was supposed to love you unconditionally . . . and not even she did. Isn't that why you always pushed people away?"*

"Are you a demon or my therapist?" *Yes! There was something there, and it wasn't just darkness.* But every step I took closer to it seemed more haggard than the last.

"Your sarcasm, your foul language, even your drinking,

you use all of it to keep others away from you. And why? Because you think that even if they get to know you, they still won't love you ... just like your mother."

"Yep, you got me," I groaned, as I struggled forward. *It was definitely an altar!* "My mother never loved me, now I'm a loner . . . Bravo!"

"But you still so desperately want someone to know you, the real you, and love you," the voice was getting stronger, talking faster, like it knew I was getting closer to the altar. *"For a time you thought that might be Daniel, didn't you? But it wasn't, he never knew the real you. He never understood."*

"Oh, you got me again," I could see the box! Shit, I was so close, and although I tried to lift up my arms to reach out, it felt like something was pulling them back. I knew I needed to continue to fight, to resist, even though it would have been so easy to just give in.

"So you wrote a book, filled it with everything you've ever felt. All your fears, your insecurities, because you hoped that there would be someone out there who would read it and understand. Someone who would finally understand how you really felt inside."

"Oh, how mother-fucking insightful!" I cried out in pain as I struggled to raise my arms; then they slowly started to rise. I was so close...

"But you couldn't even do that!" Her words seemed to vibrate within me. *"No one would even publish it, all those rejection letters, all those people telling you no. Do you know why, Riley?"*

"No!" I shouted as my fingertips grazed the box's rough edges. "Why don't you enlighten me?"

"Because . . . alone, you are not good enough!" The voice was practically shouting. *"Alone, you will never succeed! Not in anything! You need me, Riley! Without me, you will always lose!"*

"Maybe," I shouted as my fingers wrapped tightly around the box. "But I would rather fail a million times as myself than succeed even once being someone else!"

"No!" The voice within me burst as I opened the box. Inside, something was moving. *No, throbbing?* It was a deep red with veins throughout. It looked like a chunk of meat. Meat with a pulse. *A heart . . .*

"No!" I looked up to see Dolion trying to get to me, his dark eyes wide with the sudden realization that I literally had his existence in my hands . . . "This . . . isn't possible!"

"Yeah." I laughed as I grabbed the heart from within. It was warm, alive, and moving within my hand. My movements were fluid again, the voice was gone, and even the cold of the room had disappeared. "Honestly, I'm surprised myself." I threw the heart to the ground and stomped down on it as hard as I could. As I felt it flattening beneath my foot, I heard Dolion cry out. The room filled with a blinding light. A tremendous force flung me back, slamming me into the ground.

***

I opened my eyes to a wide, empty room. Disorientated, I stood up slowly, wondering if this was what Lawn always felt like. I glanced around – the altar was there; the box was on the ground and so was ... the squashed heart. *Gross*. Dolion was unconscious on the ground nearby. I approached slowly and cautiously. There was a chance this was still demon Dolion and not human Dolion. I touched his arm.

"W-what?" He was now human again, his voice timid and quiet. The silver fox was no more"Where am I? What happened?"

"Hey, the name's Riley . . . so, you know how you sold or basically handed your body over to a demon? Well, I got it back for you." I patted him on the head. "You're welcome."

I left him there, still looking dazed and confused. As I walked down the street, more confused-people exited houses and started to wander about. I ignored them and went right inside my in-law's place. They were on the ground by the door when I entered, it looked like they were just waking up. They still looked way better than they had pre-demon possession, but they had lost that certain otherworldly charm.

"Sup." I leaned against the wall and crossed my arms, "So, how does it feel to be unpossessed? Good, or is it like the worst hang-over ever?"

"R-Riley?" Lena looked at me with clear confusion on her face. "W-what happened?"

"Well, you made a deal with demons and got all possessed and shit. Lucky for you, you have, at least for now, a badass daughter-in-law who apparently can kick demon-arse.”"

"I don't understand." Frances cupped his face in his hands. "They said they would give us everything we ever wanted, as long as we gave them our souls. But the latter was supposed to come after we died! They weren't supposed to take our bodies!"

"Yeah, well, next time, get that in writing," I scoffed.

"D-Daniel!" Lena shot up and grabbed my arm, "Where is he? We told him all about this! Did he . . . did he . . . "

"Yep, I gathered as much." I removed my arm from her grip. "And he tried to rope me in as well, so thanks for that."

"We never wanted him to bring you into this," Lena snapped. "We never liked you."

"Yeah, I know.” I couldn’t hide my smirk.

"So where is he?" she pleaded.

"Daniel? Don't know. He could still be possessed, or he might not be.” But don't worry, I'll find him." I turned, walked back toward the front door, and gripped the handle. "And when I do, I'm divorcing his ass.”

***

I called for a car as I made my way toward the front gate. People were all around, clearly panicked, and confused, but I didn't really care. All I could think about was getting back to my apartment, taking a shower, hugging Andrea, and pouring myself a whiskey.

The car was there when I exited the gate. I climbed into the back and glanced up to find a familiar pair of eyes peering back at me through the rearview mirror.

"Oh!" I said, as I went to pull a cigarette from my pocket but found only an empty pack. "You, from before! Old Spice guy! Remember me?"

"Riley, how could I forget?" he mumbled. "And my name's Henry, you can see it on the app, you know?"

"Yeah, sorry," I said, chuckling. "I'm bad with names."

"Not too great with people, either," he said, but in an almost teasing way. "I hope you take no offense to this, but are you okay? You look like shit."

"Feel like it too," I said, chuckling. "Hey, do you smoke? If you have one, I'll give you five stars and a twenty-dollar tip."

"Cash?" he asked.

"No, sorry." I flashed him a soft smile. "Don't have my wallet with me."

"S'okay," he said, studying me from through the mirror, then he reached into the glove compartment and threw me a pack of menthol smokes. I hated menthol but beggars couldn't be choosers. "I don't usually let people smoke in here."

"I'll give you a twenty-five dollar tip."

"Miss money bags over here," he chuckled as he started the car.

I lit up the cigarette, taking in a long, drawn-out drag. And even though it was menthol, for some reason, it was the best tasting cigarette I had ever had. Silence and smoke filled the car for a few blocks, till he finally asked, "So what happened to you?"

"Well . . ." I leaned my head against the car window, watched the trees and houses buzz past. Then I chuckled, "You know how in-laws can be."

EPILOGUE

Welcome to Riley's Excellent and Not-at-all Fake Exorcism Service, How Can We Help You?

"Don't you think we should have at least talked about the name before you launched the website?" Andrea said, frowning.

"Or hung those posters on every street corner in Manhattan," Lawn said, shaking his head.

"I don't get why you don't like it?" I crossed my arms. "It's a great name."

"It's a bit of a mouthful," Andrea said, sighing.

"More than a bit," Lawn said, leaning back into the couch cushions. He was looking at the website I had made on his laptop, which was resting on the couch's armrest because Cat was curled up on his lap.
Thomas was standing by the balcony doors, watching Lawn with envious eyes, which made me roll mine.

"And you shouldn't have anything about it being fake in the title," Lawn continued thoughtfully, with a finger resting against his chin. "That'll make people think it is fake."

"That's just stupid," I said, rolling my eyes. "Why would telling people it's not fake make them think it is?"

"Well," Andrea replied slowly. "It's just . . . it seems like you're trying too hard to convince people that we are real . . . you know?"

"I don't know," I pouted. "But whatever . . . I bought the domain name, I registered us as a private company. What's done is done."

"You could have at least put our names in there as well," Lawn said, with a sigh. "Or better yet, had no one's name in there at all."

"A name adds a human touch," I snapped defensively, as I poured myself a drink at the mini-bar. "Besides, we're using my apartment as a home base, so it should be my name."

"You could have done Riley & friends or something cute like that," Andrea suggested.

"No one wants a cute group of friends handling their demon issues," I said, sipping my drink. "We're not like Scooby-

Doo and those teens."

"Their group was called Mystery, Inc," Lawn said, smirking. "Which is a nice, simple, and catchy name."

"Well, I'm sorry!" I huffed. "But I like it! And, you know, that out of all of us, I'm the only one who has exorcised demons before! So I think I've earned the right to pick our name!"

Andrea and Lawn looked at each other as the room filled with silence.

"Well, I like the name," Thomas chirped.

"Of course you do," Andrea grumbled. "You like anything and everything Riley does."

"Well, that's true," Thomas winked at me, and I rolled my eyes. It was definitely our thing.

"And you don't even have our prices on here." Lawn gestured toward the screen of his laptop. "It says the price will depend on the situation. What does that mean?"

"Well, I mean we can't charge the same for, like, a single possession as we would for a mass possession like in Lilith's Gardens," I explained.

"Still, we should give a ballpark figure."

"Or not charge at all," Andrea chimed in.

"Nope! Not gonna happen," I said, shaking my head. "Momma got a fucking Manhattan apartment to pay rent for. Momma needs cash."

"Momma?" Lawn cocked his brow. "Are we supposed to

call you that now?"

"I wouldn't mind that," Thomas said, grinning.

"Oh lord," I said, flopping down on the couch next to Lawn. "Please forget I ever said that."

"Okay," Lawn smirked, "Momma."

"Ew." I elbowed him, which caused him to shift slightly, waking up Cat, who cast me a scowl and hissed.

"I'm just saying, I feel weird about taking people's money for this," Andrea continued. "I mean, we're going to be saving people from demon possession . . . how do you charge for that?"

"How do you not?" I fired back. "We're going to be putting our lives at risk."

"Try to think of it this way," Lawn reasoned. "Doesn't the church, in a way, also save people from demons?"

"I guess so," Andrea said, nodding.

"Not really," Thomas frowned.

"Shhh," Lawn held up a finger to Thomas, then turned his attention back to Andrea. "And they take donations, don't they? They have expenses, they have to be able to self-sustain, just like we do. So, try to look at the money we get from people as . . . donations."

"Yeah," she said, smiling softly. "That makes sense, I guess."

"Damn, you're good," I mumbled under my breath, and

this time Lawn nudged me with his elbow.

"Well, before she gets here," Lawn said. "Maybe we should decide on a price?"

"Nah," I said and sighed, shaking my head. "I want to hear more about her situation and then decide. Also, I want to see what she looks like, you know, where she's from, what her job is."

"Why is that important?" Lawn looked at me questioningly.

"Well, if she's, like, middle class or lower, I'm going to charge her less than if she walks in here with a Gucci purse and a small dog in it."

"Riley, we can't charge people based on how they look!" Andrea exclaimed with wide eyes. "That's discrimination."

"Eh," I waved my hand dismissively. "It's not discrimination if they're rich, I'm just being opportunistic."

"Riley, I think it's better to have a set price," Lawn pushed. "If you charge everyone differently and it gets out, people you charged a lot for our services might come back and ask for refunds."

"Who cares?" I rolled my eyes. "If they do, we make up some bullshit about how the demon they were dealing was a level five demon and that's why we charged them more."

"I just don't think it's right to judge people on how they look," Andrea said, staring down at the floor.

"It's not how they look, really. It's more about what they

wear, if they have a job or if their trust fund babies or whatever. I mean, if a homeless person gets possessed, are we just not going to help them because they can't pay us our fixed rate? That's why for someone like that, maybe we charge them a penny, and if someone flies in on a mother fucking helicopter, maybe we charge them a million bucks. And that's why the website says the price will depend on the situation."

"And who will determine the price," Lawn asked. "You?"

"Well, yeah. I mean my name is in our company's title."

"Riley," Andrea started to protest.

"Raise your hand if you've ever successfully exorcised a demon." I lifted my hand high into the air. Everyone else just looked at me, hands down. "Exactly, case closed."

"That's not really fair," Lawn half chuckled. "Remind me to exorcise the next demon so you can't keep doing that."

"Sure, if you're not passed out, I'll remind you."

Before he could deliver a comeback, there were three knocks on the door. We all looked at one another, then I jumped up from my seat, straightened my clothing a bit, tucked my hair behind my ears. Turned around once more, giving the room a thumbs up.

Then I cleared my throat and opened the door, before introducing myself, "Welcome to Riley's Excellent and Not-At-All Fake Exorcism Service, how can we help you?"

Damn, it is kind-of a mouthful.

ACKNOWLEDGEMENTS

I want to thank my mother and sister for reading and re-reading my book a countless number of times. To all my friends who I forced to take time out of their day to help me, you also have my gratitude. To my editor April, thank you, for polishing my shit into a beautiful diamond. And finally, my husband, for putting up with all of my craziness while I was working on this, I love you. You have the patience of a saint. I don't know how you do it.

ABOUT THE AUTHOR

Sophie Queen

Has been telling fantastical stories from the time she was a little girl. A ravenous reader of classic gothic novels and has an unhealthy obsession with cheesy horror flicks. She has written a collection of unique short stories and even a poem or two. This is her first novel, though certainly not her last. She lives with her husband, cat, dog, and sixty-five fish in an old (haunted) Victorian home.